A DOG AND HIS BOY

By

T.F. Pruden

Hardcover Edition
Published 2021
by
Solitary Press
a division of
1986041 Alberta Ltd.

Pruden, T.F. (Ed.). (2021). A Dog and His Boy (Hardcover Edition).
Amazon, USA: Solitary Press.

This novel is dedicated to my late brother Val Thomas for the inspiration and to my teacher and friend Brian Mackinnon for giving me the tools.

For Puppits

Part One: Dogs & Boys

Chapter One

The boy crouched beside the big poplar tree with the twenty-two-caliber rifle shouldered and sighted. He reminded himself to relax as he waited for the first partridge to emerge from behind the spruce trees thirty yards upwind in front of him. The words of his father passed through his mind. He inhaled, ready to squeeze the trigger under his finger and not to pull on it.

The dog sat a pace behind the boy and to his right. He waited in silence; his gaze fixed on the trees across the swamp. The birds would soon move from behind them, and the boy would kill them. Then he could do his job. The boy, who he loved, rewarded him with the entrails after he finished dressing the birds. This was a secondary concern as the dog sought only to please the boy and lived to see him happy.

Tommy Parker though not yet thirteen years old had been hunting on his own for over two years. He lived at an isolated Manitoba ranch with his younger brother, his father, and his uncle. His responsibilities included providing meat when the men were too busy working to get to town.   Tommy was proud of his ability to do his job. The dog was the love of his life and constant companion he had bottle fed and slept with as a puppy. He awaited the command to retrieve in silence.

He was a Labrador Retriever, black and heavily muscled at eighty pounds. His intelligent brown eyes and shining coat were those of a much prized and well-fed pet. His name was Puppits. He had been a gift Tommy was shocked to receive from his father when he returned to the ranch after an extended drinking binge. Tommy loved the six-week-old puppy at once. Younger than his brother Davey's mixed breed named Doggits the hastily granted and age specific moniker had stuck. After an early squabble or two established a pecking order the puppy learned to follow the lead of the older dog. Soon they too were fast friends.

The dog and the boy had walked northwest via the rough dirt trail leading away from the homestead toward the western hayfields of the Parker family property. After crossing two sets of fence line and traveling less than a mile they continued along the trail as it turned south. They climbed the first of the rock infested sand ridges bordering the quarter section of the family property Tommy had helped to clear and fence. Topping the low ridge, they turned off the marked trail. They used the three-strand barbed wire fence at the edge of the field as their guide and walked another half mile south. They had turned east into the wind. Slowly they picked their way through the red willows and scrub oaks sprinkled among the black poplar and moved into the trees. There, among the spruce trees surrounding the many small and dry swamps dotting the ridge, hid the fat partridges they were hunting.

His brother waited for them to return to the two room cabin they called home with meat they could eat for lunch. Tommy had fried the last four eggs and slathered the remains of their bannock with margarine for breakfast. He divided it equally with his two years younger brother before leaving with Puppits in search of their next meal.

They had been alone since their father and uncle departed five days earlier for the village of Hodgson. The hamlet was twenty miles across country and just over thirty-three by gravel road to the south of the homestead. To replenish the food stocks and pick up parts for the aged baler had been the 'official' reason. The machine now awaited repairs, broken down and forlorn, east of the red painted tack shed in the front yard.

Tommy knew the men were on a drinking binge and would return only after their supply of ready cash to fund it was gone. The harvest had yet to be taken off, so he was reasonably confident of the binge ending soon enough. As the week was now over, he hoped they might arrive with food today. By now he had learned there was no guarantee with a drinking man. As he and his brother needed to eat no matter when the men should return, he decided to poach a few partridges for lunch.

A low growl from his stomach reminded him he was hungry. He took another deep breath and waited for the bird to move into the open. The single shot rifle he had bought for himself with the proceeds of his winter trap line two springs earlier was loaded with a twenty-two short. The sound of the wind rustling through the trees should mask the sound of his first shot. He planned to wait for both birds to appear before shooting the trailer. There was a chance the lead bird would be spooked by the thrashing of its mate. It might even escape before he could reload and kill it. He held a second shell between his lips for that purpose. The sour taste of the copper jacket on his tongue was helping him ignore the growing hunger.

The wind gusted and as it whipped through the swamp he smiled, knowing the noise of it would mask the first shot. He was confident he could reload quickly enough to down the lead bird before she knew her partner was dead if the gust held. His smile broadened as the first partridge emerged from the cover of the spruce. She pecked at the ground, oblivious to the hunter crouched downwind waiting to kill her.

The wind gusted stronger, and Tommy felt a chill move through him as he remembered the nights spent sleeping in the box car in the city with his brothers. They were on the run and in the care of his two teenaged half-brothers then. Davey was not yet four and Tommy only six and all of them lived in misery on the streets. Their mother, having left their father and suffering the ravages of depression and alcoholism, proved unable to care for either herself or her children after moving to the city. The boys fended for themselves. Without the strong will and bitter anger of their older brothers Tommy was sure he and Davey would be dead or in a government care facility now.

It was seven years ago they had run and more than five since he had last seen his older brothers. He missed them often. The older boys smuggled Tommy and Davey out of the city after spending nine months hiding from the Children's Aid Society at Winnipeg. The younger boys were then deposited on the front step of a rural aunt. Within a week they were reunited with their father at the isolated northern Manitoba homestead where Will Parker lived with his younger brother Joe. It was remote and devoid of modern conveniences like electricity, plumbing, and central heat. The boys took to the pioneering conditions with the enthusiasm of kids who had known life without hope.

The wind moaned as it passed under the spruce bluff and crossed the dry swamp surrounded by red willows and black poplar. The dog and the boy waited in silence. As the second partridge appeared Tommy sighted the rifle on the male birds' neck and waited. He planned to shoot the bird through the head. Though a hard shot it left a better chance to get the hen walking only paces ahead.

The partridge raised his head and Tommy inhaled. He centered the bronze dot of the rifles' forward site on the birds' dark eye as it located its mate. As he exhaled, he squeezed his right hand around the stock of the rifle, closing the trigger and firing the twenty-two-caliber short. He spit the second shell from between his lips into his hand and worked the bolt action to reload in a single motion. The rifle moved in a short arc and before the hen could run or lift off, he aimed and again squeezed with his right hand. A slow grin spread across his lips as he watched the pair of game birds kick spruce needles and dirt as they ended their lives on the forest floor.

He and Davey would eat well for lunch.

Turning to the friend at his side he gave a short nod toward the dying birds and the black dog leaped to retrieve them. Puppits would place them at his feet with the skin on their necks unbroken before again sitting to wait while his master cleaned the birds. After dressing the partridges Tommy would toss them into the bag he carried. It was a grain sack he had folded over and using baling twine tied around a pair of small stones at its corners formed into a makeshift backpack. The twine looped over his shoulder and held the carcasses of four birds Puppits had retrieved for him earlier.

They would eat well at least once more today no matter if the men returned from their bender as he expected or not. Tommy grinned as Puppits dropped the pair of birds at his feet and rubbed the dog behind the ears. He was lucky to have a reliable hunting partner and it always relieved him to shoot accurately.

It was a skill his father demanded he learn at an early age.

Tommy was grateful to his dad for forcing him to endure the often-painful lessons. The pangs of shame and remorse he felt when he took the life of an animal to feed himself had eased over the years but not disappeared. He remembered his father telling him this pain too was a lesson best learned early and never to be forgotten.

Chapter Two

The mid-July sun was directly overhead as Davey Parker drank from the enameled dipper. He filled it from the bucket standing on the small table just inside the front door of the two-room cabin. The clock ticking on the cupboard at the end of the room serving as their combination kitchen and living room showed his brother had been gone three hours. His stomach growled and though not overly concerned to be left on his own he would rest easier when his brother returned. Experience told him Tommy should be back soon, and hopefully he would bring something for them to eat.

The fact his brother hunted often didn't keep the butterflies out of his gut when Tommy went alone into the wilderness. Something about his being out there with no one to watch over him scared Davey, though he said nothing about it. He considered mentioning it to his uncle Joe earlier in the summer.

Concerned he might think less of him if he did, he changed his mind.

While he enjoyed his status as the youngest child and appreciated the rights that came with it, he didn't want to be thought weak by his uncle. His uncle Joe looked like the cowboys he saw in the movies when they lived in the city. Davey was sure he must be some kind of hero.

The life in the city seemed far away on most days and Davey tried his best not to think of it. His jumbled memories were hard to make sense of most of the time. The movies he watched with his brothers were burned into his memory. The westerns were his favorites and the cowboys his first heroes. He was charmed by the men riding across the screen with their beautiful horses and stubborn independence. Davey wished for nothing more than to be a cowboy himself. While the life on the movie screen was nothing like the Manitoba wilderness, he was strongly affected by the site of his uncle Joe on horseback.

His respect was something Davey prized.

The men left Wednesday morning and it would soon be Sunday afternoon, and he missed them. He was used to being left on his own with only his brother and the dogs for company. The boys had learned to take care of themselves long ago and both trusted and relied upon each other to survive without adult supervision. In fact, Davey often felt they were better off without adults butting into their lives. Other than the loving attention of the parents he sorely missed. He was sure Tommy knew as much or more about surviving in the wilderness as any adult they had met so far. Aside from his father or uncle of course, and he was almost as sure of his own abilities. If they weren't forced to go to school in the fall Davey was positive, he and Tommy could educate themselves. At least as well as any of the weak kneed and lily-livered schoolteachers there ever had.

Davey didn't like going to school despite scoring marks placing him at the top of his class. Proud his brother had also been cited as an outstanding student he was sure they were both smarter than any of the kids that went with them. What he couldn't figure out was why they were forced to go. They were plainly beyond the level of the teaching there. This opinion: not shared by either his teachers or his father, he reminded everyone within listening distance of when forced to go.

His father heard about it each weekday morning of the school year when Davey woke to catch the bus to take them to the vile place.

Once there he enjoyed his studies and the friends he had made as much as the sports he played. He was surprised to find he looked forward to going back in the fall though he told no one, not even Tommy, he felt that way about it.

He returned to the table where several of his pencil drawings of horses, cattle, and cowboys lay spread upon it. Davey knew he was making progress and looked forward to showing his father his latest work when he returned from town. He enjoyed the drawing and was sure he would soon be as good at it as his father if he could only find more time to work on it. Glancing over to the wood box beside the stove against the far wall of the cabin he silently cursed its yawning emptiness. It ought to have been filled hours ago. He needed to fill it with the dry and split firewood waiting at the pile beside the red painted tack shed. The chore needed to be done before Tommy got back from his hunt.

The work never seemed to end here at their remote wilderness home. As he looked at the water pail sitting on the table beside the basin, he knew it needed refilling. He should get the chores done before Tommy got back so his brother could make their lunch when he did.

Yet the pull of his pencil and the wish to escape to the comfort of his imagination was tough to resist. Davey loved to draw and couldn't find enough time to do it between chores and making room for the other men in the little cabin. Sharing the tiny space with his father, brother, and uncle was hard. What he longed for was a place of his own. There he would spread his papers and pencils out and not have to move them because somebody else came into the room. Here somebody was always coming into the room to make a meal or eat or read.

He sighed and thought of the life they led in the city before his father and mother split up and things were different. Davey remembered the room he shared with Tommy there and he missed those times almost more than he could bear. He said nothing to anyone about the constant ache inside him for losing the time when they were together. There was no use saying anything because there was nothing anyone could do to bring that time back. Or make the pain inside him better. As he stood and looked out the small cabins' dirty window, he felt tears welling and his chest constrict. He gritted his teeth and closing his eyes forced himself to take a deep and steadying breath.

Davey hated himself for being weak and refused to allow himself to cry.

Only babies cried. He reminded himself of the words his older brothers whispered to him when he sobbed on nights, they hid in the empty box cars in the city. Davey was no baby and he wouldn't act like one, he told himself again. He wiped away the tear that squeezed out of his eye and onto his ruddy cheek with the sleeve of his dirty blue T-shirt.

Davey turned from the window and sat again in the metal chair to look closely at the picture laying on the tabletop in front of him. It was a drawing of a cowboy on horseback with a lasso around the hind legs of a calf and he was sure he had drawn the picture right. While his father did his best to teach him about perspective Davey thought of it as getting the sizes right. Unlike many of his earlier drawings in this one he seemed to have done it. He looked forward to showing it to his father, who appeared to take as much pleasure in Davey's drawings as he did himself.

The memory of his mother and the surprise registered on her face when he first showed her one of his drawings returned to him. A day before Christmas and with Davey just three he presented her with the crude sketch of a star-topped tree with a family seated around it opening gifts. It was the second Christmas the family would spend without his father in their home, and she surprised Davey with her reaction. She gasped and pulled him close to her after seeing it, hugging him and telling him she loved him through tears coursing down her cheeks. After wiping her tears, she whispered to him she loved his picture. She told him he had a talent he must never deny, and one day would be a great artist.

Davey was surprised by her response and it was one of few memories he had not forgotten as he grew into an older child. His mothers' tears gave him an early appreciation for the power of art. Her affection and support of his efforts inspired him to continue drawing. It became his boy's passion and a pursuit he never tired of no matter where he should find himself.

Davey loved to draw pictures of all kinds. He scarcely had time for schoolwork or chores or even friendships aside from his beloved companion Doggits because of it. His life became a series of interruptions as he was forced into activities he considered hardly worth his time. It seemed only he knew there were so many drawings to be made. Davey was constantly searching for blank paper and a place to sit undisturbed. There he would sketch one aspect or another of life and the world surrounding him. He filled notebooks, covered walls, defaced the margins of textbooks, and destroyed countless magazines and newspapers with constant doodling. All to find an outlet for images that crowded his young mind to overflowing.

Davey checked the clock before picking up the number two pencil. He added the hint of a shadow to the face of the cowboy in the picture. There ought to be time enough to add the branding fire and the man holding the iron before his brother returned. It might cut it close, but he was sure he could fill the wood box and get fresh water before they got back. Doggits would surely bark a warning long before

Puppits and Tommy made it to the yard. When he saw the new picture Tommy wouldn't be mad at him if he didn't finish the chores anyway. As the thought fleeted through his mind he returned to working patiently at the drawing once again, determined to get the sizes right.

Chapter Three

The dog sat next to the poplar tree in front of the boy. He waited for him to remove the guts of the two freshly killed birds he had retrieved and placed at his feet. The boy would clean the birds and reward him with the warm meat before they set off for the next stop on their mission. He licked his lips. The dog was proud of his ability to help the boy secure the meat and he loved to retrieve for him. Pleasing Tommy delighted Puppits above all else. Payment for his work wasn't required, but he enjoyed it very much.

The boy leaned the Remington single shot rifle against the poplar tree, butt down and with the chamber empty and the bolt open. He was careful not to damage the front site by resting the barrel against a knot on the trunk below it. His dog sat beside the tree waiting for him to clean the dead birds. His clear brown eyes registered the knowledge that Tommy would give him their internal organs as reward for his job well done. The boy smiled at the dog and the dog licked his lips in reply. Puppits nodded to the carcasses at the boys' feet as though encouraging him to get started. Tommy slipped the twine holding the handmade game bag over his head. He laid it on the ground a couple of feet away from the partridges and prepared to clean them.

He leaned over to grasp the hens' legs above her feather tufted feet. Taking one leg in each hand he shook her dead body as he stood so the wings spread away from her torso. Bending again he lowered the bird far enough, so her head and neck rested on the ground. He placed the balls of his feet on the second joint of each of her wings, close to her body and preventing him from standing. Tommy raised himself slowly upright; carefully pulling the body of the dead bird up with him as he straightened. With an almost imperceptible easing of resistance, he felt the skin of the bird begin to detach just below his hands. He then stood rapidly, pulling the hen up and away from the ground while pressing down with his feet on her wings. In an instant he was standing with the hen's body, devoid of skin, feathers, and wings, grasped in his two hands.

Tommy transferred the birds' ankles to his left hand. He drew his four-inch folding buck knife from the sheath on his hip with the other. With great care he expertly flipped the razor-sharp blade open with his thumb before gripping the handle securely with his fingers. He kept the blade facing down and away from his body. Tommy kneeled and laid the now skinless bird on its back in front of him. Still holding the feet in his left hand with the knife he made an incision below the tiny ribs. He closed the folding blade by pressing it against the thick sole of the work boot on his right foot and returned it to the leather sheath. Into the opening he reached with three fingers and roughly pulled out the still warm entrails of the dead bird. He reached into the open incision again, using his entire hand this time and scraping with his fingers to get the last of the remains out of the cavity. Tommy separated the internal organs on the ground in front of him before tossing the heart, gizzard, liver and kidneys to the dog. The remains of the birds' skin, feathers, and offal he left for the local magpies.

He transferred the carcass of the hen into the improvised game bag. Tommy grasped the feet of the male bird and quickly repeated the process of skinning and cleaning it. Again, he fed the warm organs to the patiently waiting dog.

The boy watched as the dog devoured the fresh meat and smiled as he thought of Puppits when he first met him. The pup had been taken from his mother too early. He was only six weeks old when his father removed the tiny ball of mewling black fur from his shirt to give to Tommy. His eyes were barely open. He was frightened without his brothers and sisters and the safe warmth of his mother. The puppy whimpered as he crawled beneath his shirt collar. His father had reached into a coat pocket and removed a clear glass baby's bottle which he handed to his son. He grinned as he told him he better get it filled if he was going to feed his dog. Tommy's heart had soared. He rushed to the grocery bags on the table with the pup still squalling under his shirt to find a can of condensed milk. He punched a pair of holes into one of the tin cans with his buck knife. After filling the glass bottle, he retreated to his bunk with the tiny puppy.

The small dog grasped the nipple of the bottle without hesitation and drained the thick and semi-sweet contents. He stared all the while into the green eyes of the boy providing him with the life giving and deeply satisfying liquid.

Puppits had been his constant companion since that moment and spent the first night in his bunk. He slept there until he was past six months old when his father would no longer allow it. Tommy had bottle fed him until he was old enough to eat the freshly killed meat, dry dog food, and table scraps they gave the older dog. The puppy had grown fast and within a year was twenty pounds heavier than Doggits. When fully grown he outweighed the older dog by thirty pounds of solid muscle. In spite of the disparity in size he would conduct himself and always be thought of as the 'junior partner' among the two dogs on the ranch.

Tommy loved Puppits and they were together most times other than when sleeping or while the boy was at school. Puppits loved the boy and hated the arrival of the school bus in the fall as it took his beloved Tommy away from him five days out of seven. The dog lived to serve the boy who loved and prized him. Tommy lived to be with the dog that accepted and loved him without question.

After wiping most of the blood on his hands onto the dead leaves at his feet the boy stood and shouldered the game bag. It now contained six identically prepared carcasses of the Ruffed Grouse known as partridges among the local hunting population. He picked up the rifle and nodded to his dog, now finished eating the internal organs of the game birds, and indicated it was time to go. His brother would be hungry awaiting their return and the better part of an hour of walking remained before they were home. He wondered if Davey had been able to tear himself away from his drawing long enough to fill the wood box or fetch a pail of water. A grin played across his lips and he felt his doubt rise. His little brother was a talent all right, he thought as he smiled, but he sure left a lot of chores for Tommy.

Today was the fifth day since his father and uncle had left for town and they were out of most everything including food. The partridges he killed this morning would have their breasts removed and their legs cut into segments. After coating them in the remains of the flour he planned to fry them in the cast iron skillet with this mornings' bacon grease. The meat would be served with boiled new potatoes pulled from the garden before making the fire. If the men didn't arrive with grub soon, he planned to hike five miles across rough country to Poplar Lake. There he should find a few ducks to shoot for dinner. While it was easier to kill the ducks with the twelve gauge pump the single shot twenty-two was less likely to be heard by the local game warden. Hunting out of season was frowned upon outside the local reservation and the lake like their property was miles from there. Puppits could easily retrieve the ducks from the lake though it would take some 'bellying up' to get in range. The twenty-two shorts ought to be quiet enough for him to get a pair of them before the shooting chased them away.

One way or another they would get by until the men made it home from their latest bender with parts for repairing the broken-down baler. Eventually they should arrive with an assortment of store-bought canned goods, cured meats and staple foods. The need for Tommy and Puppits to engage in the illegal poaching they both enjoyed would end. With nothing said about it after a day or two they'd get back to work. The boys could then return to the life of chores and growing up in the isolated wilderness surrounding them.

Tommy turned away from the little swamp and walked roughly northeast. The rising mid-summer sun elevated the temperature in the heavy undergrowth of the poplar trees, scrub oak and red willows. The stunted birch and deadfall beneath the canopy of the larger trees made for slow going. Soon he reached one of the many well-traveled livestock trails crisscrossing the property that would ease the trip. His brother waited for him to prepare their midday meal and it was yet a long walk home. It had been a successful hunt and the partridge were good eating. He licked his lips as he thought of the fried meat and the new potatoes soon to come.

The dog passed around the boys' legs as they reached the hard-packed earth of the livestock trail. Puppits knew the hunt was finished. He was now free to enjoy an easy trot down the worn path leading to their home. The mornings' work was done, and his boy was safe in his charge.

Chapter Four

Davey took a deep breath. He looked at the newly drawn picture on the table in front of him with a critical eye that was rapidly becoming practiced. A cowboy standing beside a fire pulled a branding iron from the flames burning in front of him. The sparks flying above it imparted a surprising realism to the pencil drawing. Though a familiar ranching moment he was trying to capture it wasn't easy. He was pleased that he had managed to get the sizes of the different characters in the picture right to his eye. He looked forward to sharing the drawing with his father when he returned. With a grunt of satisfaction, he collected the assortment of papers and pencils from the table. They would be transferred to the cardboard box under the iron bunk beds he shared with his brother in the bedroom of the two-room cabin.

The bedroom was in fact a granary. His father and uncle had pulled it against the back side of the one room cabin the two men shared before the two boys arrived some years earlier.

The original one room building was sixteen feet wide and twenty feet long. It was equipped with a four by two-foot single sash window centered on the east wall of the clapboard one story structure. An inner screen door was paired with an outer storm door centered in the wall at its south end.

The building was not insulated. Though its open two by four-inch studs and the three-quarter inch tongue and groove pine walls were covered from floor to ceiling in heavy black roofing paper.

The pine floor was finished with cheap green linoleum. A square door with a ring lift cut into the center of the room provided access to the four-foot-deep and six-foot-wide root cellar beneath it. The cast iron cook stove sat against the west wall beside the wood box located just inside the front door. A low table supporting a pair of two-gallon water buckets and the white enamel wash basin stood across from it against the east wall. The walls and the ceiling behind and above the stove, including the exit for the stove pipe, were covered in galvanized tin. It was nailed to the surface to help prevent a catastrophic fire.

Across from the wood box on the east wall were mounted a collection of hooks. These were positioned in a pair of lines high and low used to hang the coats and outerwear of the men and boys respectively. On the floor beneath them was stored a variety of seasonal footwear. There was a roughly built cabinet mounted above the basin with a mirror on its door serving as a medicine chest. Here was stored shaving equipment belonging to the men and the toothbrushes of the boys with a variety of first aid and medical supplies.

The heavily worn and white painted rectangular table where Davey sat to draw was surrounded by four metal framed kitchen chairs: two on the long side and one at either end. It sat against the east wall beneath the cabins' lone window.

Two banks of hand-built floor to ceiling cabinets, each with plywood countertops roughly made and unpainted, filled the north end of the small cabin. They stood on either side of an open doorway cut into its back wall. Along the west wall between the cook stove and the cupboards sat a dilapidated sofa, brown and heavily worn, that served as a combination lounger and reading room.

The low ceiling with its two in twelve pitch was not insulated, and the two by four rafters and three-quarter inch pine of the roof sheathing were exposed. The ceiling unlike the walls wasn't papered.

Circling the entire room where the ceiling met the walls were arranged an unbroken line of carved wooden hide stretchers of varying lengths and styles. These were used to dry the skins of fur bearing animals trapped during the long months of the cold winter. The furs were sold in the spring and the scent of their drying permeated the poorly ventilated cabin. The men living there had grown accustomed to the greasy odor. Though he found the smell disgusting each time he entered Davey said nothing to anyone about it.

Gathering the papers into a loose stack he picked them up from the table. He was careful not to bend or tear any of the pictures as he took them into the common bedroom.

He placed the stack of drawings onto the lower of the iron bunk beds that stood against the west wall at the back end of the converted granary. Built of the same three-quarter inch tongue and groove pine lumber as the original cabin, the former granary was both narrower and shorter than the front building. At fourteen feet wide and eighteen feet long, its construction featured a four in twelve pitched roof. More of the green linoleum covered its pine floor. The makeshift bedroom was equipped with a pair of two-foot square single sash windows positioned in the middle of its long walls.

It was, barely, better lit than the front room.

The windows while dirty allowed Davey to see well enough. He arranged the new drawing carefully in the almost overflowing cardboard box he pulled from beneath the lower iron bunk. His fathers' double bed sat against the east wall across from the bunk beds. His uncles' single bed was placed against the same wall just inside the bedrooms' entrance. A big wood burning tin heater sat across from his uncles' bed and against the west wall near the front of the room. An empty wood box stood beside it. The walls behind and above the stove and the area where the stove pipe exited the building were covered in sheets of galvanized tin. The metal was nailed in place while the uninsulated interior walls wore the same black roofing paper as the original cabin.

Against the north wall at the end of the room and between the bunk beds and his fathers' bed sat an aged four drawer wooden dresser. It held clothes belonging to Davey and his brother. At the foot of his fathers' bed was another worn cabinet where both he and his uncle stored their socks and underwear. Across the corners of the room above each of the men's beds lengths of wooden dowel had been nailed to act as makeshift closets. A variety of clothing belonging to the men hung upon each of them. The ceiling of the bedroom was unfinished, and the two by four rafters and roof sheathing were exposed as in the front cabin.

While too young to remember it, Davey heard stories told by his brothers and even a few from his uncle Joe about the 'old place'.

It was where the family once lived beside the Fisher River. It had been a two-story log house built by his father with the help of his brother and home to the family when Davey's parents were first wed. Located miles south of where they now lived, he didn't remember the place. When he asked about it, he was told they lived there when he was an infant and Tommy had been a toddler.

The 'old place' was never talked about in the company of his father by anyone in the family including his uncle Joe. Davey understood it had been a beautiful home that his father had taken much pride in presenting to his mother. Spoken of in reverential tones when rarely mentioned, it was source of a great deal of pain to his family.

To him the place was shrouded in mystery. As he grew older, he was tempted to ask his father what made everyone behave so strange when the 'old place' was mentioned. He had yet to find the right time to do so. Davey hoped someday he could, as he wanted to hear the tale from his father. The 'old place' seemed to be from a different world than the one they lived in now. It seemed much like the movie cowboys that filled his dreams.

The preoccupation with preventing fires shared by his father and his uncle Joe seemed rooted in the 'old place'. It had burned to the ground long ago. Being too young to recall the event meant it had little effect upon him, but Davey knew both his father and his uncle took the threat of them very seriously. The men felt so strongly about it he was not allowed to make fires inside of the cabin, though Tommy had already been doing it for a couple of years. Davey wasn't bothered by the ban. Having watched the task more times than he could remember he was sure he could manage it should the need arise. Like many of the thing's adults kept from children he believed himself more than able to deal with fire. As it saved him from yet another chore, he went along with it.

He smiled to himself as he stood and turned away from the bunk beds and walked into the front room of the two-room cabin. His brother would return soon, and Davey decided to surprise him by doing his chores. He grabbed the water bucket at the front of the table and lifted it high so he could empty the contents into the pail behind it. The second bucket was almost filled. Taking the empty pail, he walked outside to stand on the low wooden step in front of the door. He was momentarily blinded by the brilliance of the late morning sun. Doggits rose from where he lay in the shade of the red painted work shack ten feet west of the front door to join him. The dog trotted to his side and nuzzled his free hand, tail wagging in anticipation.

Davey rubbed his dogs' ear and smiled at him before giving a nod toward the well three hundred yards north of the cabin. He stepped off the low deck. The dog followed along at his side, content to be with his young master and always ready to enjoy a walk in the sun.

Chapter Five

Tommy followed the livestock trail through the spruce trees and up the low hill behind the barnyard a hundred yards west of home. Though still cool in the trees he knew that the mix of oppressive heat and high humidity would soon make activity of any kind a chore. The fire needed to cook lunch would leave the cabin too warm to be inside of for hours afterwards. He quickened his pace. There was work to be done before he and Davey could eat and his stomach grumbled that it wanted food now, not later.

Ahead of him Puppits burst from between the trees. He barked once, loud enough to let the horses lazing in the shade of the big poplar trees surrounding the barnyard know they were coming. It also alerted Doggits to their arrival. The older dog sent a single bark in return and he bounded off toward the sound of it. Tommy was left in the distance behind him as he rushed to help himself to a drink.

Emerging from the spruce trees Tommy approached the top of the small rise behind the barnyard. The outline of the stable he helped build during the summer break from school the year before entered his vision. It was a four-stall building with an asphalt shingled roof pitched two feet in twelve. It had a two by six pine lumber floor with split doors on both sides of the building. The heavy spruce logs used to build it were chinked with moss and whitewashed, and the squat stable measured twenty-four feet square. The upper and lower split entrance door; crafted from the same two by six spruce lumber used for the floors, opened at the south end. A similarly constructed door on the north side led to a small rail fenced corral where they stored a supply of hay bales and a bin for oats.

The hay and oats were fed to teams of horses housed in the stable. The work season that began in early fall lasted until after the ice on the lakes surrounding the family property melted late in the spring. Their neighbors long ago had abandoned horses for mechanized equipment. His father and uncle persisted in using the animals for most of the work performed on the ranch during the winter months.

They used a pair of two horse teams for logging and cutting fence posts. This was done legally via permits obtained from the local forestry office or by stealing them from crown lands northwest of their property. The teams were well trained and the talk of the local horsemen as well as the pride of his father and his uncle Joe. More than a dozen heavy horses wandered the property along with an equal number of saddle horses. They were easily outnumbered by over a hundred cow-and-calf pairs. It was a rare occasion when animals other than the working teams were housed in the little stable.

The horses wandered the pastures with the cattle and were treated as pets by all members of the clan. As each of them aside from the youngest colts were broke to either the halter, saddle, or harness, little effort was needed to catch them should the need arise. Actual need was rare. Despite standing orders to exercise them as much as possible during the summer it was a weekly ride at best for most of them. They were a fat and sassy remuda as a result.

The stable also served as the primary household for the dozen cats freely roaming the property. Their official charge was keeping the rat and mouse population under control. With two breeding females at his disposal the enormous yellow tomcat who called it his home returned each fall to winter in the stable. There he enjoyed the hot meals provided to his wives and their always growing supply of kittens. Tommy's father often cursed the wandering cat, known as 'the General', for getting underfoot. He also regularly accused him of being a useless thief who didn't do his job. Yet he could be found in the stable on winter mornings affectionately scratching the frozen stubs of the big toms' ears. Few mice and never a rat would be found alive on the property. His father made sure the cats were fed at least once daily during all months of the year. The feed boxes in the empty stalls were filled with straw so they had a warm place to sleep through the winter cold.

As he passed through the barnyard the spring colts surrounded him in the vain hope Tommy might dole out a serving of oats. He scratched the cheek of a soon-to-be gelded paint yearling and rubbed the chin of a spring born buckskin filly as he passed. The growl in his belly demanded he not stop today. He walked down the hill toward the two-room cabin along the wide trail leading to the stable. As the ramshackle construction of the family home came into view he smiled.

The exterior of the cabin was as roughly unfinished as its interior and even less pleasing to the eye. A granary functioned as their bedroom. It was a well built two by four lumber framed clapboard structure featuring wood shake shingles on its moderately pitched roof and unpainted. The granary's front door had been removed and the little building dragged to sit tightly against the rear wall of the original one room cabin. There a chain saw cut an entrance through the wall, effectively joining the two. A gap between the structures was stuffed with an assortment of rags for insulation. It was then covered with pieces of rough cut two by six lumber that were left unpainted. The now two room cabin was surrounded with a two-foot-high by two-foot-deep wall of topsoil. Packed tightly against the building it was given a roughly level surface. Upon this was placed a double row of straw bales. Changed in the fall after harvest, they surrounded all save the south end of the cabin and the front door. The soil and the bales provided the only insulation from the winters' bitter cold and were surprisingly effective. Despite it the blankets of the men and boys routinely froze to the walls of the bedroom in the coldest months. The original cabin with its lower pitched roof was covered, from its roof to its improvised foundation, in asphalt roofing shingles of a dull rust color. Long ago they had been a bright red. While the former granary featured windows cut into both long walls, the original cabin made do with a single window on the east side.

The picture presented by their home was comic. The ramshackle and hurried construction was plainly meant for short term use when little time had been available for serious building. Tommy knew the men had lived in the original one room cabin for some years before he and Davey arrived. The boys had now lived at the ranch for a further seven years. He was forced to accept that the place; not so fondly known by its inhabitants and their neighbors as 'the shack', must be viewed as their permanent home.

Further down the hill he passed a shallow eight-foot-long trench dug fifty yards east of the barnyard. It was slowly filling with waste and they called it the slop pile. Here each morning they dumped the contents of the five-gallon pail which stood beside the cook stove. It was home to household waste unsuitable for burning. The shallow pit was covered over and dug again a few feet further up the hill every few years. It gave off a smell unlike any Tommy had encountered elsewhere. He gritted his teeth and wrinkled his nose as he hurried past the growing pile of filth.

Fifty yards to the south and visible through the trees sat the outhouse. It was a two-seat affair emitting its own foul stench for which he recently helped his uncle Joe dig a new waste pit. Dug five feet deep through rocks and sand, moving the building onto the new pit and covering the old one was a chore repeated every few years. The latrine was painted white in stark contrast to the unpainted cabin, the better to find it on moonless nights his father had told him. Secretly Tommy believed the paint a work of pure sarcasm as the privy was both exceedingly well built and meticulously finished.

In summer the hole beneath the tidy clapboard structure was regularly the target of powerful disinfectants. Yet the wrong breeze however slight delivered an odor to the shack that left the inhabitants scrambling to get out. As the boys soon came to appreciate, life without the wonder of modern plumbing was somewhat less genteel than the cowboy movies led them to believe.

As he walked toward the shack he wondered if he'd find the wood box full. He might have to fetch water and carry wood before making lunch. Tommy smiled at the thought of his younger brother working on his latest drawing and realized he didn't care. He was sure Davey was gifted and if it meant waiting a few minutes longer to eat it was worth it. The time was needed for him to work at his talent. Though he had composed the odd poem and even tried his hand at writing Tommy was sure that like his father he would work for a living. He would likely work with his hands and probably with his back though he earned high marks at school. At first, he was surprised when the thought hadn't bothered him. On this day like many others, he looked forward to seeing what Davey had drawn while he was hunting.

Puppits bounded up to lick his hand as he reached the red painted granary functioning as their workshop only feet from the door of the shack. Tommy grinned at the friend who was his pride and joy. The relieved satisfaction that accompanied a successful hunt arrived with him. His love for the dog was almost matched by his appreciation for the retrieving skill that made Tommy a better hunter. Together they provided meat for the family's table. The boys would eat soon and then he could decide what the rest of the day held. Whether it meant hunting or staying out of the way of the men when they returned made little difference. No matter how it went he looked forward to spending it in the company of his beloved dog.

Part Two: Men & Women

Chapter Six

Will Parker stood under the stinging hot spray of the shower and felt the heat clear the alcohol induced fog from his aching head. He reached for the bottle of shampoo standing on the edge of the tub. He squeezed a large dollop into his hand and rubbed the soap into his still thick red hair. The shower was a rare luxury, and he was enjoying it while he had the chance. He worked the soap into a lather. Will realized that until arriving five days earlier it was two months since he last enjoyed a thorough cleaning. Life on the ranch was dirty and the lack of running water limited them to sponge baths. They were no substitute for a hot shower.

He had enjoyed the comforts of the home provided by the woman he'd been seeing through the last year for too long. Today he must return to the ranch. His reserve of cash money was now drunk away. The groceries purchased on credit when he arrived in the village would be loaded into the trunk of her car. The four of them; his younger brother Joe and the women they were keeping company with, could then make the hour plus drive to the ranch.

They would leave as soon as he finished eating breakfast.

He had enjoyed the five-day party but as he sobered a sickly remorse filled him as he thought of his boys alone in the wilderness. Will was a fit and vigorous man only forty-five years old. The needs that required tending if he were to avoid becoming too crazy to function, he couldn't explain to his sons.

The knowledge did little to assuage his guilt at leaving them alone.

As he reached for a bar of soap, he silently thanked the god he didn't believe in for the precocious nature of the boys. He was grateful for that and the lack of child welfare enforcement in the wilds of the Manitoba Interlake district. Despite it being nineteen seventy-one the encroachment of civilization had so far been limited to provisioning electricity and party line telephones to the rural villages. Few paved roads and even fewer social service agencies extended beyond the capitol city far to the south. For this he was also grateful. Will knew leaving kids his sons' age alone in the wild was a crime in places where the rules of modern civilization were enforced. Despite a well-earned reputation for outrageous behavior, he had no wish to either run afoul of the law or endanger his sons.

Will grinned as he thought of them. They were in less danger alone at the ranch than when forced to live on the streets of the city after he and his wife separated. They were surprisingly mature for kids their age and could provide themselves with the necessities of life without adult supervision. He reminded himself that being forced to survive on their own for a few days would help to build their rapidly strengthening young characters. The notion comforted him though as he rinsed the soap from his eyes, he knew it was time to return home.

After breakfast he would leave for home without further delay.

The woman whose home he shared had been widowed for several years. She worked as a waitress in the Royal Hotel at Hodgson, the village closest to his property where he conducted most of his business. Ten years younger and childless, she shared a two-bedroom bungalow a mile south of the village with her younger sister. The sister was a clerk at the local forestry office and had shared her bed with his brother Joe for almost two years. While his own lack of a divorce prevented talk of permanence to his relationship, he had lately grown concerned his brother might decide to marry the woman. He didn't know if it was genuine concern or jealousy at the root of the feeling. As he reached to turn off the shower the idea that both affairs had run too long for anyone's good passed through his mind.

Will pushed the thought away as he stepped out of the shower. He grabbed the thick cotton towel, freshly laundered, soft and smelling of lilac, from the vanity counter. The boys again entered his mind, and as he rubbed himself dry, he looked into the mirror in front of him. Will noted the wrinkles on his forehead and at the corner of his eyes that weren't there when his sons arrived almost seven years earlier. He had been a younger and angrier man then, still bilious at the breakup with his wife two years before that. He was more than surprised on the spring morning when his brother-in-law Cal Thompson arrived at the ranch. Cal told him the two boys had been left on his doorstep. Cal was married to Will's favorite sister Kate. Though his sister fed and cleaned the boys they waited anxiously for their father to collect them.

He promised Cal he would be ready to pick them up in three days, and without further conversation began to prepare. His brother Joe had been equally surprised by the sudden turn of events. It was soon clear they shared a similar level of excitement at the prospect of the boys coming to live with them. After a short discussion of their new circumstance the brothers together undertook the changes to their living arrangements that seemed right.

They selected the newest of their personally constructed granaries to graft onto the back end of the one room cabin they shared. The brothers would create more living space for the new arrivals. A day of cleaning and disinfecting the granary was followed by the covering of its interior walls with heavy roofing paper. They removed the granary's front door and hitched it to their Massey-Harris model forty-four tractor to skid it into position. A window was roughly measured into the west side of the building. Joe had expertly cut the two-foot square into the side of it with a chain saw. He clambered inside the now former granary and used the saw to carve a door into the rear of the original cabin. Then he rough cut a second window into the east wall of the new bedroom. While his older brother had tended to the insulation and grafting of them together Joe dealt with hanging windows. He also finished the floor and the entrance between the two buildings. Together they cut and fastened the galvanized tin onto the wall and ceiling where they would later place the potbellied tin heater to heat the room. Will held the ladder and Joe marked the location for the chimneys' exit on the inside of the granary roof.

Those tasks had consumed the better part of a full day.

The next morning, they hooked a wagon box to the old tractor. They drove three miles east on rough dirt roads to the ranch of their neighbors Hank and Dorothy Huggins. There they purchased a set of iron bunk beds with mattresses and the pair of worn four drawer dressers from the Huggins' bunkhouse. Another two-mile drive over three more ridges of rock infested dirt trail brought them to the recently built home of their neighbors Ben and Ivy Fisher. They purchased the tin stove and pipe they would use to heat the new bedroom from the Fishers' old house. Also purchased was the old brown sofa from the Fishers' former living room. The furniture along with the stove and pipe they loaded carefully into the wagon box for the trip home. In spite of the long day when they returned with their just acquired goods, they reassembled the contents, along with their own beds, in the former granary. They had grinned at one another with a mix of relief and satisfaction as they inspected the freshly assembled bedroom.

The next day Will departed for the gravel highway then located three miles south of the homestead to meet Cal and his boys. Joe remained at the ranch applying the finishing touches to the new bedroom. Both men had been beside themselves with excitement though it was difficult to notice if one didn't know them well. That it was a momentous occasion both men understood.

Their lives would soon change in ways more significant than either of them could appreciate.

With a deep sigh Will Parker finished drying himself and hung the towel on the rack beside the shower. He sat on the cover of the toilet bowl and dressed. It was now almost seven years since that day, and his boys were growing up fast. As he pulled the grey woolen socks onto his feet he wondered when, or perhaps if, he would grow up himself. The realization stung him, and he recalled his wife, knowing their separation had been his fault as surely as he sat there.

Will knew there was nothing he could do about it, now or then.

He returned to dressing himself and resolved to get home and tend to his boys as soon as he had eaten breakfast. Before the afternoon was over, he'd be home, and he and Joe would get the baler fixed tomorrow morning. They would return to making hay for the winters' feeding and to getting the boys ready for another year at school.

He stood and looked again at the still fogged mirror at his reflection, critiquing his physique for a moment before winking at himself. The wrinkles weren't too deep yet and in his own opinion he still cut a mighty fine figure of a man. As he stepped from the warm bathroom he grinned as the smell of frying bacon and fresh coffee drifted from the kitchen to greet him.

Chapter Seven

Joe Parker lay in the queen-sized bed and listened to the sound of the shower running in the bathroom across the hall from the bedroom where he lay. He heard the women preparing breakfast in the kitchen further down the same hall. Despite the ache in his head, he looked forward to getting into the shower. To eat a meal prepared by someone other than his brother or himself would also be good.

He glanced at the alarm clock ticking on the nightstand, pleased and a little surprised to note it had just passed ten o'clock in the morning. Considering the party had lasted five days he was impressed to be moving so early. His latest hangover appeared to be of the milder variety in spite of the headache. With a glance out the window to his right he could see a clear blue summer sky above the tree line. His brother would be eager to get back to the ranch.

Joe stretched and yawned, enjoying the languorous comfort of his girlfriends' soft and clean bed. Tonight, he would return to the scabrous and sweat stained reality of his single bunk and the hard-edged reality of life on the ranch. Covering his face with the down comforter he inhaled the faint scent of lilac and the lingering aroma of the young woman responsible for his being there. He felt a jab of regret that he would soon be forced to leave the rich comfort of her home. As he considered the feeling the idea that staying longer might risk something far more dangerous than comfort rose within him. Joe had no interest in securing an impingement on his freedom. To leave today after breakfast would be best. To not return for another month or two would also be wise. Before the young beauty who owned the clean and too comfortable bed might consider him angling toward a more permanent arrangement.

Joe had been seeing the young forestry clerk Amber Hardy for the two years since she returned from school in the city to live with her older sister Audrey. Her sister waitressed in the Royal Hotel and most conveniently was the current paramour of his older brother Will. A blonde haired and blue-eyed younger copy of her raven-haired older sister, Amber was a knockout and talk of the local countryside when she returned from college. Joe was pleasantly surprised when she made her interest in him known while he was at the forestry office to secure a burning permit two springs earlier. Not a man to pass on an opportunity to experience the pleasures of the flesh he responded quickly to the enticement. Within weeks they began a torrid affair.

He was known as a cool hand with the ladies.

When word spread the young Hardy woman was keeping company with Joe Parker, the local bachelor population had been vastly disappointed. Stories of his conquests were many and the legend of his endowment local folklore. Joe made sure both were exaggerated to the extent that competition for his attention among the ladies in the community remained healthy. The field being limited due to population as well as geographically dispersed it was imperative his reputation precede him. He tried always to be sure his talent, if not his actual physical stature, lived up to the expectations of those who experienced it.

Joe enjoyed his wandering eye, and it was accepted in the community. As he was rumored to have been involved with several ladies now married to local ranchers it limited his close friends. Living on an isolated property with an older brother he considered his best friend he wasn't bothered by either the rumors or the dearth of buddies. The truth was he had spent many an enjoyable afternoon in sweaty trysts with the local beauties, both single and married, and said nothing about it. That word of his conquests had spread he considered a shame, as given the size of the community it restricted his opportunities.

Undeterred by the long running dalliance with the twenty-four-year-old Amber Hardy he was also engaged in an affair that had lasted more than five years with his neighbor Hank Huggins' wife Dorothy. As his brother occasionally slept with the same woman and had for at least ten years he considered this to be of no consequence. In addition to Mrs. Huggins, he regularly fornicated with her nineteen-year-old daughter Irma, a young woman whose talent between the sheets he discovered when she was but sixteen years of age. His inability to wean himself away from the girl despite the danger associated with the secret affair now concerned him.

Despite being thirty-one years old Joe knew he couldn't withstand the increasingly persistent advances of the seventeen-year-old daughter of their good neighbors Ben and Ivy Fisher for much longer. The nubile Georgia Fisher was a ginger haired model of physical perfection and her growing curiosity was slowly getting the better of him. Though not given to bouts of introspection he wondered if it was the danger that attracted him or if he suffered an obsession with youth.

His drive to explore the carnal delights had remained constant since his introduction to them. This was courtesy of then forty-five-year-old village seamstress Mrs. Alma Murdock when he was but thirteen years of age. Joe had delighted in furthering his experience since the summer afternoon of his initiation. He had arrived at her home to collect an assortment of his fathers' repaired work clothes. While surprised by the advances of the older woman his body responded to her touch at once. He joyfully indulged in her lustful teachings through the decade that followed.

He smiled as he thought of the many women kind enough to share their bodies with him because of the education gifted to him by Mrs. Murdock. Joe would always be grateful to the kindly woman who gave him his first experience. He remained fond of those he had explored since though he held no interest in settling down with any of them. The sexual revolution of the nineteen sixties allowed him to enjoy such a variety of physically satisfying experiences it seemed a fools' errand to limit oneself to a single partner.

While he said nothing about it, he considered his older brother's marriage to be a colossal error in judgment. He wasn't surprised when Will and his wife separated. Like himself his brother was a healthy fellow with a strong interest in the ladies. Will had been a tomcat while a young man despite coming of age during a period of greater moral restraint. Joe knew his brother was anything but the marrying kind and though he wanted to say something about it before the wedding as the kid brother he could not. He was sure Will's desire to marry was driven by his experience of the war in Europe, as he returned a different man than the one who left. His brother was an outgoing and good-natured fellow who enjoyed a party and the company of as many women as he could find before his departure. He was taciturn and given to violent outbursts when he came home. Joe was sad when the marriage fell apart though not surprised when it did. He believed his brother like himself would be best served spending his life a confirmed bachelor.

That he was gifted with the two nephews as result of his brothers' marriage he would always be grateful for, and Tommy and Davey were the twin apples of his cynical blue eyes. Joe had thrilled at their births and was ecstatic when they came to live with them on the ranch. He had delighted in teaching the boys horsemanship, hunting, and the various ways of the ranchers' life since their arrival. His brother allowed him to act as second father to his sons and he appreciated it more than he would admit. Joe assumed he loved the boys as though they were his own. Their addition to life on the ranch also removed any thought of marrying and settling down he might someday have entertained. He was grateful to them for this too though he would never breathe a word about it.

Joe sighed as he heard the running water stop across the hallway and the sound of the shower curtain rings being moved by his brother. Will would be dressed and ready for breakfast momentarily and he would join him once he enjoyed a hot shower himself. His brother was sure to be in a hurry to leave after breakfast. The twenty-six-ounce bottle of Canadian Club saved from last nights' party he planned to nurse during the drive. The whisky should prevent his hangover from getting worse while ensuring he enjoyed a long nap once they were home. It would also take the edge off the course sheets covering his single bed he knew would be plain after five nights enjoying the comfort of his girlfriend's soft mattress.

The boys had been alone too long despite their rapidly growing maturity and unassailable survival capabilities, and it was time to go. He looked forward to seeing their faces light up when they arrived and felt limited remorse for having left them alone in the wilderness for so long. They would be good and capable men when he and Will finished raising them and learning to make their own way could in no way do them harm.

He rolled into a seated position on the edge of the mattress and steadied his mildly spinning head by placing a calloused hand on the night table. He grimaced as the room wobbled and prepared for what he hoped would be a refreshing shower.

Chapter Eight

Will Parker held the ceramic mug steady in his thick fingered hand as Audrey Hardy filled it three quarters full of the steaming black coffee. As the blue-eyed woman turned to fill the cup held by his brother, he placed the coffee onto the table in front of him. Will broke the paper seal surrounding the cap on the twenty-six-ounce whisky bottle. He spun it off and poured the tan liquid into the mug until it neared the rim. Will reached across the table and filled his brothers' cup to a similar level before replacing the cap and placing the bottle on the table between them. He stirred a teaspoon of sugar and a small amount of canned milk into the over filled mug and waited as Joe prepared his own serving of the 'hot punch'. Will raised the cup to toast him over the table already cleaned of their just consumed breakfast dishes and cutlery.

"Hair o' the dog to ye bye-o," he grinned at his brother and winked as he raised the mug to his lips and drank.

"An' back at ya' hoss!" Joe said before drinking.

"Time to be gettin' home," Will said as he rested the heavy mug on the table in front of him.

"Absolutely," Joe agreed, smiling happily as the whisky warmed his stomach.

"Me cash is almost done," Will said, "we'll havta gas up Audrey's car with purple when we get to the ranch."

"I'll get 'er did soons' we get there," Joe replied.

Will Parker smiled at his brother and helped himself to another swig of the delicious 'hot punch'. The breakfast had been excellent. With his desires sated the whisky would soften the feel of his lumpy bed. It should also calm the hangover now threatening to erupt from inside of him.

"The boys'll be out o' grub by now," he said, "tho' I bet a dollar to a donut young Tommy's fed partridge guts to a dog 'is mornin'."

He smiled and pride swelled in his chest as he thought of his eldest son and the unerring accuracy of his shooting eye. Tommy was already as good a hunter as any grown man including himself and he was, justifiably he thought, proud of his ability. The skill had been taught to the boy by his father of course, and he was confident his sons hadn't gone hungry during his extended absence as a result.

"Not a bet I be takin," Joe replied with a grin to his brother, "that Puppits'll eat good and so'll Davey-boy s'long's Tommy's got ammo!"

"Reminds me," Will asked, "I grabbed two boxes o' .22 shorts and two boxes o' .30-30's but didn't get no shotgun shells, we got plenty?"

"No use fer more fer a while yet anyway," Joe answered, "we oughta be good with what we got 'til season opens."

"Miss Audrey loaded up our grub awreddy," Will smiled and raised his mug, "mus' be time to hit 'at trail."

He emptied the contents in a single gulp.

"An' a dusty one 'tis," Joe grinned across the table at his brother, "bes' get another shot o' hot punch into us 'afore hittin' it."

Will laughed and dutifully grabbed the carafe to fill his brothers' proffered cup half full of the strong coffee. He filled his own to the same level and watched as Joe topped it off with the whisky. He added canned milk and sugar and stirred the contents together.

"Guess we'll be drinkin' the rest o' that soldier straight," he said.

"She's a long drive," Joe observed, "an' it be good company."

Will chuckled and winked at his brother before raising the cup to drink.

Audrey Hardy and her younger sister Amber appeared at the door of the kitchen. The women nodded to one another knowingly as the men sat drinking at their table. Amber walked over and sat on Joe's lap, taking a small sip of the whisky laden coffee. Audrey grabbed the now empty carafe from the table and placed it into the sink. She removed its top and emptied the contents before rinsing it with hot water from the tap and placing it upside down into the empty dish rack beside the sink. The kitchen like the rest of their home was spotless clean. As she turned back to the table, she grabbed the empty mugs from the men and rinsed them before placing them on the rack beside the carafe.

"Are you ready to get moving honey?" Audrey asked as she turned to face Will seated at the table.

"Good to go darlin'," Will answered, his ruggedly handsome face grinning at her.

She couldn't resist stepping to the table to kiss him deeply on the lips. The taste of the whisky laden coffee on his tongue spurred the need for him inside her.

Will grasped her around the waist and pulled her onto his lap, swelling instinctively and wanting her. Audrey giggled as she pulled herself away and stood, straightening her blouse and instinctively touching her hair.

"That'll be enough of that," she said, before adding with a grin, "for now."

Will smiled up at her from the kitchen chair.

"Time to go," he spoke softly, his voice low, "me boys been home alone too long."

"Yes, they have," she answered, "too long."

"We'll gas you up when we get there," he said, "I'm too broke to pay Stanchuk to do it 'fore we leave."

"I've got plenty to get there," she replied.

"Good girl," he smiled as he answered and winked at her.

"Well, pard," Will said to his brother, who was messing with Amber Hardy across the table from him, "let's getta' hell outa these girls' way so they can get back yar' an' get themselves ready fer' work tomorra'."

Joe smiled at Amber as she rose from his lap and stood, straightening her clothes.

"Souns' like a plan brother," he replied, "Miss Amber is tired 'o me anyway."

Amber shrieked and slapped playfully at Joe's shoulder as he stood.

"You cut that out mister," she said, "you know damn well you have no interest in stickin' 'round town, much less stickin' with me!"

"Oh darlin'," Joe replied with a laugh, "you know you're my best gal!"

Will stood and laughed, grabbing Audrey and pulling her to him as he picked the whisky bottle from the kitchen table.

"If only I were the only one!" Amber replied smartly to Joe.

She kissed him lightly on the lips before spinning on her heel to walk out the door to her sisters' car parked in the driveway beside the house.

Joe made no reply, grinning ruefully at Audrey and Will as he followed her to the car.

Will pecked at Audrey's cheek before grabbing his hat and following the young lovers out. He climbed into the front passenger seat of the car while Audrey locked the door. Amber and Joe were in the back seat, play fighting and laughing together, and Will grinned as Audrey slid into the drivers' seat. She smiled back before starting the nineteen sixty-nine Caprice and shifting it into reverse. She backed up the short driveway and turned onto the deserted gravel road leading from the village to her home. Will spun the top off the whisky bottle and took a long swig. He tuned the AM radio in the cars' dashboard to the country music station broadcasting from Portage la Prairie and removed his hat. He was ready to go, and it was a long drive to the isolated ranch.

The gravel road ending at his front gate had not been there when the boys arrived seven years earlier. He was forced to make repeated presentations to the provincial transportation department at Fisher Branch to have it built. His boys were school aged. Without a highway to the homestead, he was required to transport them three miles across rough country each morning to meet the school bus. It passed the east end of their property on its way to the school at the Peguis Indian Reservation. While he preferred to have the boys educated at the provincial school in Fisher Branch the only bus operating within reach of their isolated property served the Reservation school. He was grateful the boys were allowed to attend it. The alternative was to have them live in foster care during the school year and his sister housed them the first winter they lived at the ranch. He had sworn to bring them home no matter the cost when told of his boys' misery at being forced to live away from their bachelor family.

It took the help of his sister and the pioneering ranchers whose respect he had earned as a veteran to prevail upon local Reeve Darwin Gansler. The need for the poorly maintained and regularly unpassable gravel highway was eventually recognized. Within two years of the boys moving to the ranch the road was built. His sons were then picked up at their front gate for transport to the Peguis Central School each morning, weather permitting, like the other children living in the Harwill Postal District. Both men and boys were relieved to no longer have to rise at five a.m. for the hour-long journey to meet the school bus.

His sons had since lived on the ranch with them full time. They thrived despite the regular binges the men indulged in after Will deemed them old enough to be left alone a couple of years earlier. While the current bender had lasted longer than any of their earlier joint departures, he was confident Tommy would care for his younger brother. In fact, he doubted Davey needed anyone other than himself to survive. His sons were possessed of an unnatural maturity that rendered adult supervision all but irrelevant. While it was spooky to find them capable of managing on their own at such an early age, he was grateful for it all the same.

As he watched the countryside speeding past the window of the Chevrolet the strains of Hank Williams sad crooning emerged from the radio. He turned the volume nob hard to the right so he could hear the song above the noise of the gravel pounding the underside of the car. Will grinned and took a long pull from the whisky bottle. He passed it over the seat to his brother and harmonized roughly with the chorus of the country standard.

It had been a good party and he enjoyed spending time with the woman, but it was time to return to his first priority, which was the raising of his sons. Retrieving the more than half empty whisky bottle passed over the car seat he looked again to the passing countryside. Now rich in the full bloom of summer the burgeoning nature reflected his stubborn optimism and he smiled contently. Will was pleased with his life. He looked forward to returning to his isolated home and his rapidly growing sons.

Chapter Nine

Joe Parker enjoyed the view of Amber Hardy's tight jeans as he walked down the steps leading from the kitchen door of the neat bungalow. He crossed the driveway and slid into the back seat of the green Caprice beside her. As she leaned against him, he thought what a beauty she was and how he was a lucky man to be enjoying her company. He was reluctant to leave despite his desire to return to the ranch and the care of the boys. Pulling her close he kissed her on the lips, smiling as she snuggled against him.

"You're my sweet baby," he murmured into her ear.

"And you're my wild cowboy, Joey," she replied.

"Mos' likely won't be back in 'til we get 'at hay put up," he said, his deep voice low with a hint of sadness.

"I could borrow the car and drive out to meet you," she answered, her voice soft, "if you wanted me too."

He considered the offer for only a few seconds before making his reply.

"Meet me at the south ridge where the Ashern road meets 'ar south quarter a week from tonight?" he asked.

"Could do," Amber said, twisting one of her blonde curls around a finger.

"It's a date, be there 'bout 6 o'clock," Joe replied, smiling as he thought of the coming tryst.

"Mmmmm," her answer was a low moan, "gonna miss you 'til then cowboy."

She turned her face to his and they kissed, Joe holding her close.

"Be missin' you too darlin'," he said in the low voice.

Audrey and Will climbed into the front seats of the big car.

Joe relaxed into the back seat, removing the wide brimmed western hat he wore and placing it crown down onto the shelf behind the back seat. He watched his older brother place his own hat in a similar position on the seat between himself and Audrey, who was behind the wheel. Joe grabbed the whisky bottle Will passed over the front seat and took a long swig. The older sister backed the car up the short driveway to the gravel highway. As they pulled away and headed north toward the distant ranch contentment rose within him, and the country music emanating from the radio added to his comfort.

Holding the young woman close as the car swayed negotiating the rough gravel highway; alternately pressing them against and away from each other as it rapidly ate the miles, Joe grew reflective. Something about the closeness of the woman this morning was new and warmly pleasant, and he enjoyed being taken by it in spite of himself. While it might have been the whisky talking, he was almost willing to admit his feelings for Amber were more real than he previously allowed himself to consider. It surprised him to discover he wasn't disturbed by the idea and he resolved to ponder the matter at greater length when sober.

He had no intention of sharing this information with her.

Joe smiled as he blew one of her stray blonde curls from in front of his nose. He pulled Amber against him as the car swayed, thrilled by her tight soft skin. It surprised him again to find himself not wanting to be without her at his side.

"Damn you're fine, girl," he whispered into her ear.

"Mmmmm," she murmured in reply, "you sweet talkin' cowboy, what you tryin' to do to me now?"

"Jus' wantya to know I know honey, thas' all," he breathed, his deep voice barely audible.

She turned and looked into his now half-drunk eyes, searching them to see if he was playing with her or sincere. Despite the whisky he had consumed he remained inscrutable, and she kissed him before turning away and snuggling against him.

"Don't you go tryin' to break my heart Joey," she said.

"Never gonna do that sweet thang'," Joe whispered into her ear.

He squeezed her against him to reinforce the sincerity of his words.

The depth of his feelings surprised him, and he said no more. He silently accepted the whisky bottle passed over the seat back by his brother. Joe noted with sadness it was nearing the end of its contents.

Again, he thought of his brother and his wife. He recalled the happiness of their mother when Will informed the clan, he planned to marry the daughter of his fathers' oldest friend Ben Manson. Ben was a respected elder of the Cree Nation whose family lived on the Fisher River Indian Reservation north of the Peguis Reserve that bordered their property to the east. Like their father a veteran of the First World War, Ben was held in high regard throughout the community by the white and Aboriginal populations alike. Flo and Robert Parker were thrilled when their eldest son announced his intentions to settle down with Ben's widowed daughter Marilyn Thompson. They blessed the proposed marital union without hesitation.

Joe was surprised by his brothers' choice of his late best friend Bill Thompsons' widow as his bride. He suspected the veterans who had served together in the Second World War might have a secret pact at work behind the scenes. While outwardly happy for Will and Marilyn, to himself he kept serious doubts in the ability of the union to last.

That his brother was changed by his experience of war in Europe was undeniable, and his parents spent many nights worrying about their eldest son when he returned. Will's constant partying and violent behavior in the years following the war for a time terrorized the community and earned him numerous stints in the provincial jail. On more than one occasion he barely avoided a lengthy penitentiary sentence.

Their mother had lived long enough, just, to see Will marry. Though pleased by the union, blame for her too early demise was placed squarely at the feet of the incessant worry caused by the dangerous living of her eldest son. Will and their father grew distant after she died, and a civil word between them had been rare since Will separated from his wife.

Though his brothers' wife Marilyn was loyalty personified when Will's drinking and carousing descended into acts of violence against her, she left him. Joe was bitterly disappointed in his brother when he discovered Will had beaten his wife. For a time, a schism came between the brothers. He was hard pressed to remain loyal to his brother then, and he had been closer to Will than anyone he knew.

It was the opportunity to form the partnership on the distant ranch that healed the rift. Joe decided that as no one could know what went on behind closed doors aside from those behind them he was best served forgiving his brother the unfortunate marital failure. The fact Will lived in a painful and apparent state of personal torment since the separation eased Joe's mind about the righteousness of his decision.

The brothers never spoke of the matter.

The experience served as an object lesson for Joe.

He was determined to avoid suffering a similar fate as that meted out to his older brother, who he continued to love and respect. Plainly the harrowing world of marriage was one that could humble a man. Joe had no wish to join Will in the misery that failure of such an undertaking could inflict upon even the strongest of men. If he must live his life a confirmed bachelor to avoid it, he was, fortunately, able to secure the companionship of a woman when the biological urge required.

Joe settled into the cars' back seat after again passing the whisky bottle to his brother, noting that only a swallow remained in the almost dead soldier. He pulled Amber Hardy's lean body against him and inhaled the scent of her clean blonde hair deep into his lungs.

He wished suddenly he could keep the smell with him always.

She pushed herself into him in response and the squeeze of her hand on his knee was reassuring even as a slight dread rose in his belly. Joe wondered at the increasing madness coming over him in the company of the sweet young woman. He sighed as he exhaled, relieved he would soon be back at the isolated ranch with his brother and the two boys.

Only there was he free to return to his bachelors' life and the solitary cowboy ways he enjoyed. A little time apart from Amber would do him good. While he would miss her warmth in his bed tonight, he would enjoy the return of his freedom and his solitude tomorrow. Of this he was almost certain regardless of the uncomfortably warm feelings he was experiencing.

Joe peered out of the speeding car at the rugged country. The full bloom of summer exploded with the overgrowing life of untamed nature, and he relaxed as they drew closer to his home. He calmed as the wilderness neared. It loomed at the edges of the gravel and threatening to take back the begrudgingly granted space for the narrow road at a moment's notice. With a wan smile he noted the beautiful summer day, the sky a clear and unspeakable blue. Joe looked forward to seeing the relief on the faces of the two boys when they returned after being away for what had surely been far too long a time.

Home was just a few miles of uneven gravel away now. It pleased him to be returning to the boys with the supplies they needed and their wayward father safely in tow.

Chapter Ten

Will Parker forced himself not to listen to Joe cooing at the younger Hardy woman in the back seat of the big Chevy. The car sped through the low hills of the Manitoba countryside in a cloud of gravel dust. Low ridges intersected with neatly maintained homesteads and fields lined with fresh hay bales alternated with ripened crops of oats, barley, and wheat on either side of the highway. He grinned as he realized he was looking forward to returning to the summer of work that lay ahead of him on the ranch. The five-day party had relieved him. The peculiar madness that drove him to the carousing was again sated despite his guilt at leaving the boys alone in the wilderness. He could now count on himself to toe the straight and narrow for several months.

Soon the boys would forget he was away too long. The lives of the four men living on the isolated ranch could then return to the rhythm of work and play to which they were accustomed. He would get past his guilt and the boys get over their fear and the result should be them growing closer and stronger because of his unfortunate condition. Will repeated the thought to himself as he watched the countryside roll by and listened to the cars' radio. He swigged from the rapidly emptying whisky bottle.

With a tenderness belying the hatred he felt for himself he turned his gaze from the countryside to study the widow seated across from him. She concentrated on the road ahead of her as she expertly guided the heavy car over the rough gravel highway from behind the enormous steering wheel. Audrey Hardy remained a beautiful woman as she entered her middle thirties. Will remained puzzled that she chose to share herself with him in spite of his well-earned reputation for bad behavior. He knew it wasn't overestimating the facts to state that the widow Thomas, who restored her family name of Hardy after the death of her husband in an industrial accident ten years before, could have the company of the man of her choosing in the territory. Her husband had been the hardworking and responsible mining engineer Joe Thomas. He left insurance enough for her to retire from a tellers' career at the credit union after his too early demise. When she tired of being locked away in mourning, she shocked her family by starting a career as a waitress in the Royal Hotel at Hodgson. While working there she had met Will Parker.

Will smiled and shook his head, again confounded by his continuing good fortune with women and children. He felt in no way deserving and guessed he earned the good luck as reprieve from the demons who took residence in his head after he experienced the horrors of combat. The battle for the Hochwald Gap in the forests of Germany took place when he was a peach fuzz cheeked boy of nineteen and a private in the Lake Superior Regiment of the Canadian Army. While the women and children came and went with the years the demons like thistles, stubborn and unwelcome, remained. They tormented his nights until it seemed he must still be among the trees of the Hochwald with the shells of the eighty-eights exploding. Over and over his friends screamed in their death throws around him.

Will believed himself duty bound by the sacrifice of his buddies in the faraway forest to live out the ongoing misery of his life. He had long ago failed to deal with the never-ending guilt of his survival. That a creeping madness prevented him from keeping his marriage vows and slowly destroyed him he accepted as the fair price he must pay for his survival. His compulsion to seek the company of women damaged by the merciless vicissitudes of life he believed a just reaction to the knowledge revealed by the numbing cruelty of the terrifying days in battle.

Will now held the world and its people in absolute contempt.

He had shared his view of the world with no one since returning from the war. In truth no matter what events should transpire in his life, including marriage and the birth of his children, his vow was never to share the private horror. It wasn't honor that compelled the promise. Will had lost the naivety of honor in the stultifying cruelty of the German forest in the winter of nineteen forty-five. It was a duty to those he left behind that drove him to survive the lingering misery. He refused to share the disgust he held for the world and his fellow man despite being forced to live with it.

"You're like fine wine, Miss Audrey," he said, loud enough for her to hear him above the sound of the radio, "you get better lookin' every day."

Audrey turned and gave a quick smile before returning her gaze to the gravel highway in front of her.

"Plainly Mr. Parker," she said with the grin spreading across her delicate features, "you are no connoisseur of fine wine."

Will laughed at her sharp humor, his mood lightened by the reassuring gaiety of her optimistic personality.

"Having spent some time on the continent my dear," he answered her in his best attempt at a formal and English accent, "methinks that my evaluation of your beauty is most accurate."

Audrey laughed aloud, turning again to smile at the thickly muscled and craggily handsome man seated across from her.

"You don't need to charm me cowboy," she said, "you've already managed to get my pants off!"

Will almost choked on the swallow of whisky he was taking and laughed as he wiped his mouth with the back of his hand.

"An' I sure hope you'll be takin' 'em off fer me agin ma'am," he said to her, and winked as he reached across and softly squeezed her shoulder.

"Can I get us off of this shitty excuse for a highway first?" Audrey answered, taking a hand away from the steering wheel long enough to stroke his calloused hand.

Will laughed again, enjoying her quick wit and relieved she maintained an interest in him.

"Wha' certain'ty ma'am," he teased in reply, "an' don't let me interfere with yer' drivin!"

Audrey's laugh was sweet with innocence and Will returned to gazing at the countryside passing beyond the window of the big car. The fields lining the gravel highway were growing smaller and less regular now as the wilderness encroached further upon the attempts to impose civilization onto it. They were drawing closer to his home and relief grew inside of him as the miles passed and the rugged nature of the country around them increased. Soon they would cross the bridge over the Fisher River and just three miles later they would turn north. There lay the almost untamed wilderness of the postal district of Harwill, location of the brothers' ranch and their home.

He recalled the supplies he purchased, doing his best to reassure himself he had collected the items on the list he set off to retrieve five days earlier. The whisky befogged him, and he abandoned the effort until he was home and could look the mess over with Tommy, who created the list. His eldest son would put away the groceries and make sure the clerk at Hershfield's store hadn't forgotten anything. Little could be done in the event she had. There was no other way to make sure they weren't billed for items not purchased, and Will had decided young Tom would train to manage the books for the ranch. The boy seemed to have an eye for figures as well as a way with words.

He smiled as he thought of his sturdily built and studious son. The boy was already rebelling against his fathers' tendency to deliver orders despite an obvious wish to please him. Tommy was as headstrong and independent as he had been as a boy. Will was certain that a strong hand was the only thing to raise him with if he was to turn out a better man than his father. Though it pained him to treat the boy harshly he remembered how the heavy hand his father raised him with had taught him to toe the line. He avoided the worst calamities his nature had enticed him to as a result and he was committed to doing the same for his son. A day would come when young Tom would thank him for treating him the way he did. Though Will knew more than a few years might pass before that day would arrive.

He reminded himself that a father had to sacrifice for his son if he were to raise him to be a good man. No matter how he might want to wrap the boy in his arms and give in to his every fool desire. Will nodded to himself as he looked out the window and thought of Tommy, respecting his own father and thanking him silently yet again. He was committed to doing what he had to so the boy would know what it took to be a good man in this miserable world. Tommy might have to hate him for a while because of it, but some day in a far-off future he'd appreciate what his father had done. Whether begrudgingly or with pride one day he would, and Will hoped he lived to see it.

As the big car turned north to speed up another narrowing gravel road he smiled as he thought of how excited Davey would be to see them get home safely. The boy was possessed of the sweet appearance and fiery disposition of his mother along with her blue eyes. Will was often astounded by the stubborn willfulness of his youngest son. Raising him was proving to be a more delicate task than parenting his older brother. Will feared he was doing a less effective job with Davey than he owed him. He was routinely charmed by the younger boy.

Davey was gifted with a surprising degree of artistic talent and seemed to have an innate appreciation for it lacking in his older son. Will was regularly astonished by the ability of the boy to grasp the higher concepts of art. He would expound upon them in the still to be lost patois of baby talk that peppered his speech. Davey-boy was a mystery to his father as well as his favorite. Will knew the treatment of his sons was not only unequal but also unfair to both of them. Despite the knowledge he seemed either unable or unwilling to do anything about it, though he was unsure which. One day in a distant future he was unlikely to see the fruits of his poorly managed labor would be born.

Will hoped sincerely it wasn't to the detriment of his sons.

As the car turned west onto the narrowest of the gravel roads, they had yet traveled it began a slow climb up the steep hill leading to the Parker ranch Wills' tension eased further. His boys waited only a mile and a half beyond the rock infested ridge. Soon they would be together and safe.

Part Three: Coming Home

Chapter Eleven

Tommy wasn't sure what alerted him to their arrival first, the sound of the motor on the highway or the bark from Puppits. Whatever it was he heard them before he saw the car crest the ridge a quarter mile away. It roared down the ridge to cross the alfalfa field east of the homestead, where the azure blue seed flowers waved in the breeze.

He recognized the small block vee eight powering the sixty-nine Caprice of his fathers' girlfriend Audrey and knew shortly they would be at the front gate. The woman had a reputation for driving the big car as fast as any man dared to on the loose gravel of the local highways. Tommy had ridden with her on several occasions and knew it was both well-earned and accurate. That she made a practice of never drinking and driving he decided marked her as a woman of substance. Despite the addiction to speed he believed his father and uncle were in no danger traveling with her.

He was lying on his bunk reading, his head beneath the west window and propped on a pair of dirty pillows when he heard the car. With a sigh he placed a marker between the pages of the dog-eared paperback before stashing it carefully beneath them. Tommy rolled out of the narrow bed and strode thru the front room of the shack. Davey sat engrossed in his latest drawing. He shaded his eyes and confirmed it was Miss Audrey's car racing across the front quarter before motioning the dogs to stay. He stepped off the porch and broke into an easy jog toward the gate seventy yards northeast. It would do him no good if one of the men were forced to open it. They were likely to be half in the bag and he was sure to catch hell if he didn't do it for them.

Tommy dislodged the locking handle from the swinging wooden gate. He pushed it open and crossing the driveway to hold it as Miss Audrey hurtled toward the end of the gravel only yards east of him. He tried not to flinch as the woman locked the brakes of the big car and through a cloud of dust waved to Tommy as she wheeled into the yard. The car roared past him and slid to a stop feet from the door of the shack. He closed and locked the heavy gate deliberately, in no hurry to discover what the return of his father and uncle meant for the rest of his day.

He walked slowly toward the shack. The sound of laughter from inside the Caprice and the dogs barking at the new arrivals encouraged him. The muffled voices sounded almost sober and the women, including Miss Audrey's younger sister Amber who he had a crush on, sounded like they were having a good time. With any luck their presence and the drinking they were doing would prevent his father from being angry with him. Above all else he hated to be dressed down by his father when strangers were present. He considered anyone who didn't live on the ranch to be a stranger. Silently he hoped his father was in a good mood.

Tommy stopped as a spring colt and her bay-colored dam wandered up to him in search of a scratch. He rubbed the mare behind the ears and tickled the soft lips of her buckskin stud colt.

Again, he reviewed the list of chores he was responsible for while the men were away.

The pigs had been fed twice daily and kept locked in the pen north of the big corral that reached almost to the well three hundred yards north of the shack. He made a smudge fire for the mares and their colts each afternoon, and the latest example was smoldering and surrounded by no less than a dozen of them now. The water troughs he pumped full several times each day. First thing in the morning, at midday, and again before dinner each night to make sure the animals always had fresh water. Earlier he filled the Coleman lamp with 'high test' gas and hung it from the nail driven into a rafter in the front room of the shack. It waited there, ready for lighting when the sun slid behind the ridge west of the barnyard. He had split enough of the dry poplar they burned in the cook stove for at least another couple of days. The split wood he stacked with a row of billets placed bark side up on top of the pile to help keep those under it dry in case they got rain. The dishes used for lunch were washed and Davey had dried them. They were in the cupboard where they belonged. He had made his bed and straightened the blankets on Davey's top bunk well enough for it to pass inspection. The floor in the front room was swept. The slop pail was emptied the night before and less than half full emitted no more than the usual foul stench.

As far as he could tell he had seen to his responsibilities and kept the shack as clean as it could reasonably be kept.

Tommy wondered what he had forgotten, his stomach tightening and sweat beading on his upper lip. Whatever it might be his father would discover it before noticing those chores he had successfully completed. Should he be fortunate enough to have seen to his assigned tasks there would be no praise given. He sighed and swallowed his fear along with the bitter anger.

He knew better than to allow anyone to know what he thought about the lack of appreciation given to his work.

The mare turned away, disappointed to receive no oats and taking her colt with her. She headed for the blackfly relieving smoke of the smudge Tommy had made for their relief. He was left with no reason to further delay the welcome of his father and uncle. He resigned himself to his fate and turned away from the horses toward the shack where the adults were getting out of the car only thirty yards away. Tommy took a deep breath and pasted what he hoped looked like a genuine smile onto his tanned face. He threw his chest out and his shoulders back the way his father told him to and prepared to face his destiny.

No matter what awaited with the men home the pressure of taking care of his brother and running the ranch was relieved. If nothing else, it should ease the pain in his belly a little. In spite of the failings, he was sure to have committed their arrival would allow him to escape a little of the fear that seemed always part of his life. For this if nothing else he was grateful, and he smiled as he walked toward the waiting car. There were bags of supplies to be retrieved from inside of it and a list to be checked against the bill sent with them. As it was another task that was his to finish, he knew he best get to it before raising the ire of his father. It had proven nearly impossible for Tommy to avoid his fathers' anger since coming to live with him at the isolated ranch.

Chapter Twelve

Davey yawned and looked up from his latest drawing when the dogs barked. His brother rushed through the room to see who was driving across the field toward their home. He smiled as Tommy jogged toward the gate. It must be his father and uncle returning. He collected the pencils and papers from the tabletop in front of him.

He laughed aloud as the return of his father, who he called Daddits as it rhymed with the names of both Doggits and Puppits, meant the end to his worry. Davey hoped his uncle Joe, who he called Joey-Pie, would come home too, though it was a secondary concern as his father was his first concern. When his dad was home nothing could be wrong for long. Knowing he was somewhere close by, either in a field working or out hunting or doing chores somewhere in the yard, was enough for Davey to relax. His arrival meant all was right in the world. And that the boys had again survived the dark time when they were forced by the cruel circumstance of life to survive on their own.

As he picked up the drawings joy rose inside him. He knew his father would be happy to see him and he looked forward to showing him the new pictures. Davey would sit on his lap at the table and eat the cookies he brought, and they could talk about how his drawing was getting better. Davey was proud to have survived his fathers' latest absence though he wouldn't say anything to him about it. His Daddits might even be a little drunk as he sometimes was when he returned from his trips to town. He was sure to be pleased to see Davey, if less so with his brother. He was sorry for Tommy when their father directed his anger at him. Though it was good to be excused from having the raised voice and withering comments directed his way. He didn't know what Tommy did that raised their father's hackles so easily. If he could figure it out, he'd tell him and save him the misery it so plainly caused. As for himself he shared a special place with his father. Only the two of them lived there, and other people weren't allowed in, not even Tommy or his uncle Joe, and for that Davey was grateful.

Davey walked through the front room of the shack and opened the screen door. He stood on the front step as the familiar car of Miss Audrey roared to a stop in front of it. The dogs barked as they circled the car with their tails wagging hard enough to cause them to sway, overcome with happiness. He smiled as he heard his uncle Joe and his father tease them from inside the dust covered car. Together the dogs whined in excitement as they were forced to wait.

Davey thought back to the first of the extended absences he could remember the men taking and giddiness rose inside him. The scene today was almost a copy of it. Except that he had been crying with relief when the men returned then as he didn't believe his brother when told they would be back. The days apart from them the first time were a bewildering nightmare and Davey cried himself to sleep each of the two nights they were away. It frustrated Tommy who had done his best to convince him the men would soon be home. The misery he suffered that first weekend was almost more than he could bear. Davey wondered how he would ever survive such a hellish experience again when it came to its merciful end. As he stood on the front step, he smiled broadly at the people sitting in the car. A new pride rose inside him as he realized the men had been away longer this time than any. They had been away longer, and he had been less disturbed by it than he had ever been. He and Tommy had run the ranch and seen to their chores without them. He had not cried even once and barely noticed they weren't around though he missed kissing his Daddits at bedtime. The feelings that rose inside him as the realization grew were different and he liked them. Mixed with relief at seeing his father and uncle was a new awareness.

He believed himself now able to live without them.

He was amazed by the idea.

As his brother stopped to pet a mare and her colt, he had a flash of insight he was yet too young to fully understand. His brother must feel this way too. For the first time Tommy's carefully hidden disappointment and frustration were plain to him. Though still young they were no longer little boys and suddenly he knew it. As he stood on the step and shaded his eyes with his hand, he saw his brother for the first time, knowing his frustration and feeling his disappointment. His brother expected no thanks and was angry about it. Soon he would react the same way when the men returned after leaving them to survive on their own. He didn't know what it was, but as he smiled at the adults in the car something had changed.

It wasn't them, and that scared him a little.

Davey stood in the heat of the July afternoon and watched the men in the car talk with Miss Audrey and her sister Amber. His brother had a crush on the younger woman. Soon they would get out of the car to greet the boys. Something inside of him had broken loose, and without a word he spun on his heel and turned away. He walked into the shack and sat at the end of the table to watch the scene through the window.

He was surprised at himself. His habit was to wait impatiently for his father to get out of the car before throwing himself into his arms, relieved he was home and happy to see him. This time it was different and for a reason he couldn't grasp he needed to withdraw, if only for a moment, before greeting the men. Somewhere inside him bitterness rose, like bile from his stomach after eating too many fresh picked chokecherries. For a reason unknown he wanted to hide it from his father and uncle. Somehow, he knew his brother would understand. He had a powerful urge to share it with him, to tell him he got it, that he was disappointed and angry too.

Davey took a long drink from the mug of water sitting on the table where he left it. He calmed as the heat of the sun eased, his eyes adjusting to the dim light in the front room of the shack. He looked on as the men opened the doors of the car and stepped out to stretch themselves beside it. They petted the wound-up dogs and quieted them. Miss Audrey and her sister Amber also emerged from the car and stretched, beautiful and unreal in the brilliance of the afternoon sun. He watched the breeze wave their long hair. They adjusted dark glasses and smiled at the men with gleaming white teeth and Davey thought how it looked like a movie scene. The old happiness rose inside him as he saw his father and Uncle Joe were in good spirits and good health. Soon everything would return to normal, and he would be alright. What he felt was probably just the heat of the sun hitting him after being inside too long. It was passing and the excitement of seeing his Dad and his uncle Joe returned as he sat in the cool of the shack. In a moment he'd race outside and throw himself into his fathers' arms the way he always did. Then he could give his uncle Joe the hug he knew he wanted.

His momentary anger disappeared, withdrawing like the fog waiting to greet them on the front quarter in the cool mornings of the early fall. The fog always disappeared with the rising of the sun, and as Davey rose from the table the momentary chill of the strange foul mood ebbed away. It was replaced by the happiness and relief he was used to feeling when his father returned. He smiled and without a further thought pushed himself away from his chair and rushed out the door. Davey laughed and prepared to throw himself into the arms of his father, his Daddits, the man he loved best and whose attention he valued above all others.

His father and his uncle were home, and it was a bright and sunny day. They would enjoy themselves together in the warm comfort of their shared home.

Chapter Thirteen

Tommy watched the men and women climb from the dust covered green car now parked in front of the shack. His father and uncle petted the happy to have them home dogs and the women stretched after the long drive. His chest filled at the sight of Amber Hardy and he wished for a cap to shade his eyes. He feared being embarrassed and hoped the blush wasn't rising in his face. It was almost impossible to tear his eyes away from the woman.

She was the most beautiful girl he had ever seen. Over the last year he had come to hate his uncle Joe for keeping company with her and bore a secret shame because of it. He knew his uncle wasn't serious about any of the women he ran with and there were more than a few of them. In his heart he believed Amber Hardy deserved better. Tommy hated being too young to present himself to her as a suitor in his rogue uncles' stead. He hated himself for the secret wish to usurp his uncle Joe in the woman's affections. In only three weeks he would be thirteen. The miserable day would highlight the fact he was too young to show his feelings for her, though something told him his uncle Joe already knew how he felt. As the sun beat down, he hoped his dark tan would cover the hot blush now creeping up his neck. He wanted to hide and wished again for a hat or a pair of the glamorous sunglasses the Hardy women wore.

Their gaze shifted from the horses crowded around the smudge fire to Tommy as he walked to greet them. If only he were taller so he could better show off his rapidly filling out physique. He was becoming a man and girls were noticing. The thinly worn and dirty white t–shirt he wore was tight across his shoulders, straining to contain the muscles growing thick beneath it from daily labor. Tommy found out last winter that big changes were happening to his body. He panicked when he discovered a sticky wetness covering the sheets of his bunk after waking from a surprisingly realistic dream.

Tommy assumed he had wet his bed and was too ashamed to tell anyone. Instead, he waited in damp misery until his father left for the barn. He stripped the sheets from his bunk in silence and heated a bucket of water to wash them.

His uncle Joe watched bemused as his nephew said nothing and hand washed the heavy flannel sheets. He waited until Tommy returned from hanging them on the clothesline outside before addressing him.

"That weren't piss," Joe said to the boy, his voice low.

He stood at his side as Tommy drank from the dipper, he filled from the water bucket.

"What?!" he answered, plainly distressed his uncle was aware of what he had been doing.

"That weren't piss in yer blankets 'is mornin'," Joe repeated, his voice was soft.

"Whatya talkin' 'bout?" Tommy asked.

Panic rose in his chest and fear of discovery filled the pit of his stomach.

They were alone in the front room of the shack. His father remained at the barn grooming the teams of horses wintering there while his younger brother was asleep in the top bunk in their shared bedroom.

"That were a wet dream ya had," his uncle said, "means yer becomin' a man, 'ats all."

"A man?" Tommy had replied, bewildered.

"Yup," his uncle said with the gentle tone in his voice.

Joe paused a moment and listened, making sure they weren't overheard.

"Calls 'em 'wet dreams' and it means you're a man now," he continued, "gotta be careful where you stick yer pecker from now on too."

"Where I stick my pecker?" Tommy asked.

He was stunned by the words and didn't know what else to say in reply.

"Yup," his uncle's patient voice went on, "gotta be careful when you're foolin' wit dem neighbor girls 'an yer cousins too, else you'll throw a woods colt an' 'at won't do."

"I don't fool with my cousins!" Tommy had protested.

He was embarrassed as he remembered the first time, he explored his cousin Virginia. A couple of years older and very much interested in experimenting, after thanksgiving dinner a year earlier they met in her parents' car.

"Had me first time wit' one o' 'em cousins meself," his uncle Joe's voice was calm, "tain't nuttin' to be 'shamed of neither, not out here in 'is wilderness."

"But that's wrong," Tommy had replied, scared and embarrassed, "they told us that in health class at school."

"School ain't got no connection to real life boy," his uncles' voice took on an edge.

"You jus' remember to pull it out when you get 'at 'funny feelin' risin' up in yer belly,' he said, "an' fer' gods' sake spunk outside, no woods colt 'at way."

"Ok."

Tommy's reply was a croak.

Humiliation filled him. He was both stunned by his uncle's words and embarrassed at being found out.

"Nex' time I'm to town I'll bring ya back a supply o' French Safes," Joe said, his voice again soft, "you can practice gettin' 'em onto yerself when yer jackin' off so's you'll know how to use 'em when 'a time comes."

"Jacking off?" Tommy had repeated, mystified.

"Yup, 'ats when ya' pleasures yer own self wit yer own hand," his uncle said, "it's natural an' it'll help' keep you from messin' yer sheets if you jack yersef' off now an' agin."

"But where would I do that?" Tommy had asked.

Tommy's voice was also low. He was too stunned to protest.

"I use 'at shithouse meself," his uncle Joe said, smiling at the boy, "you don't think it takes me 'at long to take a shit do ya?"

Tommy had looked at his uncle standing beside him in a surprising new light. A kinship and a new respect for the man standing beside him grew.

"So, it's ok if I want to touch myself?" he asked, his voice grave.

"Course it is," his uncle replied, "it's natural and good fer a man to relieve himself, an' don't believe any jackass trysa' tell you different, you hear?"

"I won't," Tommy heard himself answer, thinking of the words of the minister in the church he attended with his mother long ago, "and thanks uncle Joe."

"Anytime kid," his uncle said, "anytime an' don't be 'fraid to ask me 'bout 'at stuff anytime ya' needa, ya' hear? Anytime."

"Thanks," Tommy had answered, still too stunned by the conversation to say anything else, "I will."

The truth was Tommy had known of his body's emerging capabilities even before the events transpired with his cousin Virginia in the back seat of his uncle Fred's car. He had been thrilled the summer before by the not insignificant experimentation carried out by Irma Huggins. While he hadn't experienced the emission he earlier suffered in his bed, he did get the 'funny feeling' his uncle Joe said he ought to be careful about as result of her ministrations. The neighbors' daughter was two years older than his cousin Virginia and more developed. Tommy was thrilled that she allowed him to explore her hard young body when they found themselves alone. Neither had he complained when she practiced orally stimulating him. He did his best to make sure they were alone together regularly after that. It confused him that she ignored him when they were in the company of anyone else, be it adults or kids on the school bus. She explained that what they were doing would be frowned upon if anyone but the two of them knew about it.

Tommy claimed to understand, not wanting the private times with her to end.

When she secured a high school aged boyfriend and lost interest in him before the Thanksgiving Dance, he was hurt. He got over it quickly when the dalliance with his cousin had begun. Virginia surprised him with the invitation after the family dinner at his aunt and uncle's farm. They had since experimented together whenever the opportunity presented itself. Tommy was now aware girls found him to be almost as interesting as he found them.

Tommy forced himself to look away from the Hardy woman. He lowered his eyes in embarrassment after seeing the smile on his uncle Joe's face as he watched Tommy walk up to the car. His uncle knew the thoughts whirling inside of his head and it shamed him, though he could see plainly that Joe enjoyed watching him squirm. Somehow the man always seemed to know what he was thinking when it came to girls. He remained grateful for his advice and for sharing his experience of certain topics too difficult to talk about with anyone else. Tommy was unnerved by his uncle's ability to know his mind almost before he knew it himself. He was convinced Joe knew he had been messing with his cousin Virginia. He might even know he had fooled with Irma Huggins, though he said nothing.

Tommy looked at the ground and almost imperceptibly shook his head as he tried to clear his mind of all thoughts related to girls. He had to retrieve the grocery bags from the trunk of Miss Audrey's car and check the bill against the items contained there. Those he compared against the list prepared five days earlier, and he needed to be in control of his faculties if he was to avoid mistakes. Mistakes would lead to the humiliating dressing down from his father he'd like to dodge. He forced himself to remove thoughts unessential to dealing with the detail-oriented task from his mind. It was difficult, as the scent of Amber Hardy's perfume was almost enough to cause him to rush for the outhouse in search of relief. With a supreme effort he raised his face to the adults standing by the car and smiled. He would tend to his responsibility despite his body no longer being fully under the control of his overworked young mind.

His father and his uncle had returned, and life should soon get back to normal. Before long the aching pressure of responsibility would melt from inside him. He and Puppits could take a walk in the cool of the trees. Crazy thoughts about girls and the stress would seep from his mind like water evaporating from a swamp in the Manitoba summer. The day would pass and the rhythms of life on the ranch soon return.

The isolation of their partnership, together and apart, beyond the judgment of strangers and responsible only to one another, could again take hold. Only then were they truly safe, in the company of their private thoughts and the silence of the wilderness.

Chapter Fourteen

Davey watched his brother walk in from the gate to greet the adults. They were stretching and talking outside the shack beside the big green car. He wondered if the adults could see the blush rise in his brothers' face as he drew closer to Miss Audrey's little sister Amber.

Would they see his growing misery?

For a moment he felt sorry for his brother, wishing there were something he could do to relieve his strange mix of shame and anger. A second later he realized there was not. His brother was growing up, as he was himself. Both were finding the troubles of the life they had led were to be replaced by new ones they would have to sort out as they met along the way. Davey was surprised by the insight, as it meant that most if not all the painful lessons, they had learned so far would be replaced by new and possibly more difficult ones. The imagined finish line he expected to find at some unknown point in his future was never to arrive if this were true. He was shocked by the idea. Davey wanted nothing more than to have things stay the same. With his Daddits home and his uncle Joey-pie beside him, there to protect the boys and keep them safe from the miserable world waiting beyond the front gate of the isolated ranch.

Why did they have to leave the ranch?

Why did things have to change?

Davey felt tears rise inside him and with an effort forced them back. He swallowed hard and steadied himself with a hand on the table. He wouldn't greet his Daddits and his uncle Joey-pie with tears running down his face. Not after surviving their longest absence without crying even once. A determination he hadn't felt before rose inside him and he smiled as he noticed his brother walking tall. Tommy's chest was thrust out and his shoulders were pulled back the way Daddits had taught them. He walked like a man. With a nod he strode forward to greet the adults. He filled with pride for his brother and himself. Davey laughed aloud as he pushed himself away from the table to greet the returned men.

"DADDITS!" he yelled with joy, "UNCLE JOEY-PIE!"

He bolted out the door and leaped from the front step of the shack and tore crazily around the car, his excitement real, and threw himself into the waiting arms of his father.

"DAVEY BOY!" his father shouted back.

He grabbed him under the armpits and tossed him above his head, catching Davey and hugging him close as he fell.

"I LOVE YOU PA!" Davey shouted, wrapping his arms around his fathers' neck and hugging him tight.

"I love you too Davey!" his father answered, pulling his face away and kissing the boy firmly on the cheek.

Davey smelled the whisky on his fathers' breath and by the sound of his voice could tell he was drunk. He smiled to himself. Now his dear old Daddits would really be eager to spoil him. His father was full of guilt when he came home after leaving them alone, and he knew how to take advantage of it.

"Tommy kept the livestock fed Pa," he said, intent on striking while the fire was hot, "and he made sure we ate good too."

"Did he?" his father replied, smiling as his youngest son went first into the defense of his older brother.

"Did you help him take care of the place or did he do it all on his own?"

"Oh, I helped," Davey said, smiling and knowing he had his father right where he wanted him.

"I did dishes an' I stayed outa trouble an' I drawed some real good pichers'!"

"You did?" his father answered, happy the boy was so obviously pleased to see him.

"Are you gonna show 'em to me?"

"Sure am Pa," Davey said.

He went in for the kill.

"Soon's we get da grub unloaded an' hava cookie ~ didja 'member tagettusa cookie Pa?"

His father laughed the half-drunk laugh and squeezed his baby boy against him.

Davey knew the cookies were hidden, like a streak of undiscovered gold, somewhere inside the grocery bags waiting to be unloaded from the trunk of the big car.

"I sure wouldn't ferget to bring cookies fer me boys Davey," his father said.

He chuckled as he lowered his son to the ground beside him.

"You give yer brother a han' gettin' 'at grub outa 'at car an' hep' yersef, you hear?"

"YAYYYY!" Davey shouted as his feet touched the earth, his glee real, "I LOVE COOKIES!"

"Hi unca Joey-pie!" he said, his greeting was shy but affectionate.

He hugged his uncle before moving to the back of the car where his brother now stood waiting for the trunk to be opened.

"Hullo Miss Audrey," Davey said.

The dark-haired woman walked with the key in her hand toward the trunk of the car where he stood with his brother.

"T'anks fer bringin' Pa an' unca Joey-Pie home safe," he said.

"Hello yourself and you're very welcome Davey," Audrey replied, smiling at the precocious boy and charmed by his performance.

Miss Audrey had no children of her own and Davey had understood she wasn't interested in being anyone's mother soon after he met her. He liked her all the same as she treated him and Tommy with a respect lacking in most adults he had known.

"You're booiful Miss Audrey," Davey said to the woman.

He meant it and was again surprised by her polished glamor.

"You look jus' like a movie star!"

When the woman laughed and flashed her perfect smile at him Davey saw he had scored again. Miss Audrey would be firmly on his side at least so long as she was going with his father.

"You're a charmer Davey," she said as she reached to unlock the trunk, "you're going to be one lucky man with the ladies, just like your dad!"

"This one's got the Parker gift Will," Audrey said.

She chuckled and looked over the car to the adults on the other side of it.

"You better keep an eye on him, or some woman is bound to steal him away!"

The adults laughed, and Davey congratulated himself while maintaining a straight and wholly innocent face. Miss Audrey had liked what he said. She meant what she said too. He could easily charm most adults. The patois of baby talk he kept up when talking to them was lost when he was with kids his own age.

He shot a glance to his brother standing beside him and gave Tommy a sly wink as he saw his knowing grin. The boys were careful not to let the adults see the exchange take place between them. Soon they would enjoy the cookies that were the intended fruits of Davey's labor. His brother was also pleased that he was keeping the mood of the adult's light with his performance.

Miss Audrey opened the trunk and returned to the conversation, whose topic was the undeniable charm of Will's boys, unfolding on the other side of the car.

Davey waited as Tommy unloaded the groceries. His brother passed him a lightly loaded paper sack to carry inside while he took two of the heavier ones. Davey walked into the shack and placed it on the table, rifling through the contents but not removing anything, knowing his brother would have to check them as they were put away. The big yellow bag of cookies he found at the bottom of the brown paper bag. He withdrew it carefully to avoid spilling the remaining groceries, a toothy grin of satisfaction spreading across his blue-eyed face.

Davey loved the crunchy oatmeal cookies. He would have to control himself or the package would be empty before anyone else got even one of them. That would cause him to be sick and on the receiving end of a dressing down from his father. For that reason alone, he must try to be patient. Triumphantly he opened the bright yellow waxed paper of the family sized bag of cookies. He smiled as his brother fetched more of the paper sacks from the car. Tommy was too busy to join him.

He withdrew the first cookie and held it to his nose, closing his eyes and readying himself for the treat. It would be too soon gone, and he must savor it. As his brother walked in and placed another pair of grocery bags on the table he bit into the cookie. The crisp oatmeal exploded into his mouth and the sweet flavor filled him with a relief found nowhere else. His eyes still closed; he murmured his deep satisfaction with the magic treat. He was carried away for a moment from the filth of the shack surrounding him. Lost in the joy of the cookie he was freed of the unspoken fear of whatever mysterious troubles life might have in store for him. Crunching happily on the small biscuit he was a boy without a concept of the guile that so often accompanied his young life. For a moment he enjoyed an innocence he had only heard was part of childhood. That it hadn't been part of his own life was forgotten as he chewed the cookie. The sweet flavor relieved him, if only for an instant, of all concern for the world outside the shack.

His father and uncle had made it home. They would enjoy the summer afternoon together, eating the delicious cookies and looking at his new drawings. All was now right in his world. Somewhere inside him he believed it always would be despite the misery that had accompanied the journey so far. He smiled happily and selected another cookie. It was the prize earned by his patient wait for his fathers' return. Davey was satisfied the frightening loneliness had been worth it. He bit into the sweet crunchiness, smiling as he chewed and looking out the dirty window at the men and women talking beside the car. All was well and again he was truly safe.

Chapter Fifteen

Tommy walked through the front room of the shack with the fourth pair of paper sacks filled to overflowing. He placed them on the counter at the end of the room. The tabletop was filled with a half dozen of the brown paper bags and more awaited retrieval in Miss Audrey's car. His younger brother sat at the table working on what must be his fourth oatmeal cookie.

"Don't get carried away with 'em cookies Davey," he said as he turned to the door to collect the next load.

"You'll be sick if ya eat too many."

"Ony ma third one," Davey replied, his mouth full as he smiled at his older brother.

"Save you some fer sure."

Tommy laughed as he walked from the dim of the cabin into the heat of the afternoon sun. His brother loved cookies as much as he loved anything aside from his dad and his dog. He hoped he didn't make himself sick or run afoul of their father.

He leaned into the trunk to retrieve another two of the brown paper grocery bags, trying not to crush them or spill their contents. Loaves of white bread protruded from the top of one bag, and he felt the weight of a heavy ring of bologna sausage waiting at the bottom of the other. Tommy licked his lips in anticipation. Tommy smiled and hoped his father had remembered to get a jar of Cheez Whiz. It was one of his favorite treats along with the 'Bung' style bologna produced by the Manitoba Sausage Company at Winnipeg.

He recalled the heavily veined sausages hung in the window of the company store on Selkirk Avenue in the north end of Winnipeg. The huge rings waited for the butcher to slice or cut them into chunks for his customers to take home. They had tormented his empty belly when they lived on the streets of the dirty city.

His father also loved the 'round steak' as it was known locally.

When he returned from a bender he liked to sit at the table with his sons and grin while they stuffed themselves. The usual meal was sandwiches made with white bread, Cheez Whiz, and the thickly sliced bologna slathered in yellow mustard. It was a rare moment of joy Tommy shared with his father, and he cherished the time spent together as much as he enjoyed the thick sandwiches.

He worshipped his father.

As he placed two more grocery bags onto the counter, he looked forward to sharing a sandwich with him. One more trip and he'd be ready to start checking the contents against the store bill. Before he knew it, he would be filling his growling belly with food killed by someone else's hand, and he treasured the thought.

Davey sat at the end of the table reading the contents of the cookie bag. He waited as patiently as he could for Tommy to finish unloading the groceries. Only after their father came inside would he have another cookie. He was impressed to see his brother demonstrating such restraint. Davey loved cookies more than Tommy loved bologna. To stop eating the treats without being told took more discipline than he thought either of them had.

"You ok?" he asked.

"Course I'm ok," Davey snapped, "waitin' fer pa 'fore I eat any more, don' wanna spoil ma' dinner."

"Probly ony' gonna have san'wiches anyway," Tommy said, "how many you had so far?"

"Ony' four," Davey replied, "trynna' make 'em last."

"Wow!" Tommy said, genuinely impressed, "Pa will be proud o' you fer' takin' it so easy!"

"Ya think?" Davey asked, his voice earnest, "cuz it's killin' me an' I want more!"

Tommy laughed as he walked toward the door.

"You watch what he says when he sees you ain't made a glutton outa' yerself' when he gets in here!"

He left to retrieve the last of the groceries.

Tommy pulled the two remaining bags from the trunk of the car, knowing the women would leave when told he was done. His disappointment that Amber hadn't said hello to him was balanced by his relief at not having to try conversation with her in front of his uncle Joe. He would be tongue tied and barely coherent if forced to talk to her with him there. Tommy was pleased to avoid the moment despite the disappointment. He walked into the shack and through the front room, depositing the grocery bags on the countertop. Two bags of dog food awaited retrieval in the open trunk.

"Ar' ya' done loadin' 'em in yet?" Davey asked.

"Atsa' last bags," he replied, "just dog food left an' Pa be in soonsa' women leave."

"Good," Davey said quietly, anticipation clear in his voice.

Tommy noticed he had resealed the cookie bag and eaten no more, determined to wait for their father before touching them again. He was impressed by the surprising maturity shown by his brother, and it occurred to him that Davey was growing up fast. He recalled that Davey had not cried at all despite their father and uncle being away longer than ever. He had also done the dishes and carried wood and water without complaint. Tommy didn't have to scold him to do the chores as he had when they were younger.

"Thanks fer helpin' out 'round here Davey," he said, "you're a good brother an' I 'preciate the help."

"You welcome Tom," Davey's reply was solemn, "you're da' bes' brudder a guy could have."

A lump formed in the back of his throat and Tommy said nothing more, instead rushing to check the trunk of the car. His brother was growing up and news of it came as a surprise despite them living so close together. It would likely be a shock to his father and uncle as well. He was stunned to realize his own growing maturity was probably going unnoticed. For a moment he was ashamed of the unspoken anger growing steadily inside him. Being so close to one another seemed to cause a kind of blindness. It prevented them from seeing each other as they were. The idea he had been unfair to his father and uncle for failing to notice his frustration or to appreciate his contributions occurred to him. The insight shook him as he wrestled the pair of heavy dog food bags out of the trunk. He took a deep breath before speaking again, not wanting to betray his feelings.

"Grubs unloaded," he called over the roof of the car to the adults gathered there, "thanks kindly Miss Audrey."

"You're welcome Tom," the woman answered, her tone warm as it always was when she addressed him.

Audrey used the more 'adult' version of his name, and he liked it.

He turned after closing the lid of the cars' trunk, picking up a bag of dog food and carrying it to the tack shed fifty feet south of the shack. Returning for the second bag he was momentarily annoyed when both dogs crowded him. They smelled the dry goodness waiting for them in the big paper sacks. He would have to feed them before getting to work on the list. With a sigh he pulled his knife as he stepped into the tack shed and sliced the top from the nearest bag. Filling a small bucket waiting on the floor beside the dog food he carried it to where two bowls waited on the east side of the small shed.

His head spun with thoughts that made no sense.

He poured the food into the bowls and replaced the pail before closing the door of the old shed. It was filled to bursting with harness, saddles, rifles, ammunition, and the various tools required to keep them in working condition.

Tommy crossed the short stretch of beaten earth and strangled grass in front of the shack and entered, planning to retrieve the list from the cabinet drawer where he left it. He stopped just inside the door to draw a breath and did his best to calm himself. It would do him no good to let crazy and unaccountable feelings mess up the job. As with each of the tasks he had completed since the men had left, he was determined to get this one done well. He gritted his teeth and reminded himself to focus, thinking again of squeezing the trigger and how he learned not to jerk on it. He smiled as the hunters' calm spread through him.

He opened the overflowing drawer and pulled the list, written in his easily recognizable scrawl on lined paper, from among the dish towels filling it. Tommy readied himself to check it first against the contents of the waiting grocery bags and then against the store bill his father would give him. The exacting task would be completed, quickly and accurately, before he enjoyed a bologna sandwich as reward for a job well done.

He heard the men saying goodbye to the women outside the shack. Soon they'd leave and the routine of life at the ranch return. Things would get back to normal, and he and Puppits could get back to enjoying the long summer of alternating work and play. Tommy smiled and took the first cans from the nearest grocery bag. He checked them off the list he had placed on the counter, hearing the wind rustle the leaves in the trees south of the shack. The rising breeze would deliver a cool evening after the slick humidity of the long afternoon. He looked forward to spending it in the company of his dog and his family.

Part Four: Fathers & Sons

Chapter Sixteen

Will Parker smiled as the big car crested the last ridge east of his front gate. Home was a quarter mile away across a field of ripening blue alfalfa. Relief flooded through him as he confirmed the grey smoke rising above the property came from a smudge fire burning in the purpose-built pen. It was surrounded by at least a dozen mares and their colts. Pride swelled his chest as he noted the dedication of his oldest boy. Tommy had made the fire and clearly the horses appreciated it. He was struck by the value of his son and reminded of the trust he placed in him.

The car swayed on the rough gravel of the narrow road. Audrey sped down the ridge and across the field toward the front gate. He saw Tommy jogging through the yard to open it before they arrived. His son would be relieved they were home Will knew, though the taciturn boy was unlikely to say a word about it. He watched as the gate swung wide and he crossed the driveway to hold it open. Tommy had made sure there were no animals near the quickly approaching car and stood waiting for it to pass. The boy would close the gate behind them to prevent any livestock escaping the yard. Will grinned as his son handled the task with the sure skill of a man.

"Looks like 'at boy bin' takin' care of 'em hosses," Joe's voice was proud from the back seat.

"Everything else too I bet," he replied.

"Betcha' Davey can't wait to get 'at 'em cookies," Joe said, chuckling.

Will smiled, knowing his youngest son was likely still working on a drawing and looking forward to seeing him. He damned himself silently for being away so long, promising in vain that he wouldn't do it again.

"Bet 'es workin' on the latest," he replied, wondering at the skill of his youngest boy, "an' I bet it's a good 'un."

"Ain't gonna take 'at bet," Joe said, "boys 'er getting' to be men quick an' we're lucky to have 'em."

"Damn right!" Will grunted and said no more as a lump pressed the back of his throat.

He waved the white Stetson at his son while Audrey slid the big car expertly through the gate. Tommy raised a hand in laconic reply as they passed. The woman wheeled the rapidly slowing car to a stop in front of the shack. Will looked closely at the horses crowding the barbed wire fence of the smudge yard. It was clear they had been watered regularly since he left. As no pigs wandered the yard, he knew his sons had taken care of them. The intelligent beasts would have dug themselves out of their pen in search of food and water if it wasn't provided. A glance to the shrunken wood pile showed the boys had kept themselves fed during his absence. Plainly they had experienced no obvious trouble caring for themselves and the animals while he was away. His relief grew as further evidence of his sons' growing independence greeted him.

"Thanks for the ride darlin'," he said thickly to Audrey seated across from him, "the boys'll be glad we're home."

"Anytime hon," the woman replied, smiling at him from behind her dark glasses, "and I just bet they will be."

'Twas a long one this time," Will said, "too long I 'spose."

"I appreciated it though," Audrey answered him in a low voice, reaching across to squeeze his hand, "and I'll apologize to them for keeping you so long if you need me too."

Will smiled at her, appreciating the sincerity of her offer and the tenderness of her touch.

"Ain't no reason fer that," his answer was genuine, "do 'em boys good to learn to survive on their own."

"I'll take your word for it," Audrey replied, smiling at him, "now let's get out of this car so I can stretch my aching back before we get back on the road."

Will made no reply, instead reaching for the handle and opening the heavy door to step out of the car and into the July afternoon. The humidity settled onto him like a topcoat as he stood. He quickly donned his hat to protect himself from the sun, almost blinded for a moment and feeling the whisky hit him. The bottle was empty, and he realized they had drunk it faster than he meant to and was momentarily dizzied. The dogs were surrounding him now and he grinned down at them. They bounced their wagging tails off his legs and whined their happiness at seeing him. Will leaned to scratch the older dog behind the ears, pleased that neither of them exhibited anything other than joy at his return. He pushed the guilt rising inside of him away.

With his brother chatting to Amber Hardy in the car he watched as his oldest son slowly crossed the yard towards them. It surprised him to see the dirty white t-shirt he wore now stretched to cover thick muscles growing in the boys' upper body. He grinned as he noticed that Tommy's shoulders would soon be the envy of most men. His son was as tall as Audrey and he had yet to hit the teenage growth spurt that should result in him matching his father. As he stopped to scratch a three-year-old bay mare and her spring colt Will could see the assurance of a well-trained horseman flow from Tommy. For a moment he feared his pride might overwhelm him.

"He's getting to be a fine-looking young man," Audrey spoke from beside him, also watching Tommy as he approached.

"Ain't 'at the truth?" Will replied with his voice low, glad to have been interrupted, "he works like a man awreddy."

"You must be awfully proud," Audrey said, "to have such a capable and trustworthy son."

"He's my pride and joy," Will's answer was quiet, "but don't tell 'im that by jeezus or I'll have trouble on my hans'!"

Audrey shook her head, knowing he meant every word of the telling statement.

"Your secret's safe with me," she said, "but don't you think it'd be a good idea to let him know how you feel about him?"

"Young stud horse needs a short lead on 'is halter an' a pair o' sharp spur in 'is ribs if 'es gonna be worth 'is salt," Will replied.

He smiled as he looked at the woman standing beside him.

"I intend to make sure this'ns worth his," he said, his voice low and plainly sincere.

"So he's a stud horse then?" Audrey asked, astonished to hear Will speak so freely, "and that's how you're raising him?"

"Damn straight," Will answered her, the smile on his face broadening, "jus' 'a same way as my ol' man raised me."

Will turned away from her and looked to the boy, who slapped the mare on her shank as he resumed his course to the car. He watched as Tommy raised himself to his full height, throwing his shoulders back and his chest out. The boy strode manfully toward the waiting adults exactly as he had been taught.

"Look at that posture," he said to Audrey, his voice remaining low, "you won't find a straighter back on an army barracks, and few stronger anywhere."

"I don't doubt it for a minute Will," Audrey replied, shading her eyes and watching the handsome boy walking toward them, "but isn't he still just a boy?"

"Mebbe 'es young but 'e ain't no boy," Will's voice was soft.

He paused for a moment as he looked at his son.

"Kid's as good with a gun as I am," he said, "an' accordin' to 'is uncle 'es getting' to know 'is way 'round the ladies too, so you bes' be careful with 'im 'er 'e might surprise ya."

Will laughed his loud and hard-edged laugh, knowing Audrey was shocked to hear him speak this way about his son. It pleased him to see surprise register on her face despite the dark glasses.

"But he's so young!" she gasped as the reality of his words struck her.

"An' 'es bin' breedin' horses, cattle, pigs, an' everything 'at lives as long as 'es been on the ranch," Will replied.

He smiled at her, enjoying her obvious discomfort.

"Be unnatural if he weren't aware o' what's what," he said.

"You're not telling me," Audrey said, mild shock registering in her voice, "the boy is active already?"

"Far as I know 'e mus' be," Will replied.

He lowered his voice further, hoping Tommy wouldn't hear him as he approached.

"Cuz' 'is uncle bin supplyin' 'im with French Safes 'fer a whal' now," he said.

"What?" Audrey said as she looked at the big man, plainly distressed by the news, "and you're ok with that?"

"Tell 'a truth 'tain't no bizniss 'o mine," Will's voice was even.

He looked at his son walking toward them, a boy becoming a man.

"Seems to me like 'es growin' up," he said in the low voice, "an' long as 'es safe 'ats what counts."

"But he's so young," Audrey whispered her protested.

"Gonna be thirteen in two weeks," Will said, "an' how old was you wenya got started?"

"Christ I was older than that," she grunted her reply.

"Pert' sure I weren't much older an' 'at myself," he replied, "don't seem like I got much right to complain, longs' 'e don't go throwin' no woods colts."

Audrey stood and stared at the boy from behind the dark glasses. It was uncomfortable to have to appraise him in the light of the new information. She said nothing while she thought over what Will had told her.

"Damn," she said, "all this time I've been thinking he was just a lonely kid."

"Oh 'es still a lonely kid," Will's answer was thoughtful, "but 'is life's makin' 'im into a man awful quick thats all, ain't nuttin wrong with 'at."

Will could see Audrey was shocked by the conversation. He stepped close and wrapped her in his arms, kissing her full on the lips.

"Now don't you go bein' 'fraid o' my boy Audrey," he said, "gotta remember 'es still my son an' 'es bin taught to respect women an' children like a good man's sposedta."

Audrey smiled up at the big man, knowing he meant every word he had said and the attraction to him overpowering the twinge of fear.

"I'll take your word for it cowboy," she said, squeezing the hard muscles of his shoulders beneath her hands, "don't I always?"

Will gave a short laugh and kissed her again.

"An' 'ats why I love you darlin," he said, releasing her.

He turned as his youngest son burst from the door of the old shack to greet his prodigal father.

The sun beat down and warmed him. His worries evaporated as he turned to greet Davey, the son he loved with a fierceness that surprised him. It was his job to protect the boy from the misery of the outside world. Will was relieved to be back at the ranch. He would soon get back to the rhythm of his life here, the only place on earth where he felt truly at home.

Chapter Seventeen

Joe Parker sat in the back seat of the big car and watched as young Tom closed the gate and began his slow walk to greet them. Though doing his best not to he could hear the conversation of his brother and Audrey. He hoped the boy was far enough away that he wouldn't. Tommy was growing up too fast for his own good was Joe's privately held opinion; though he hadn't shared it as there was no changing the fact of the matter. Life came at a man at its own pace Joe knew, and the only choice for any of them was to face it or run away. Young Tom had made the only choice his character allowed. Despite the knowledge the boy was living hard and had been forced to mature far too soon. He occasionally worried Tommy might someday be broken by the strain placed upon him so early.

"Looks like 'at kid's got the weight o' the world on 'is shoulders," he mused aloud, forgetting for a moment he wasn't alone.

"He's pretty as a picture though," Amber murmured from behind her sunglasses as she watched Tommy come toward them.

"An' 'e likes 'a ladies too," Joe replied, with an edge in his voice that surprised him, "so you be careful 'round 'im, you hear?"

"Don't tell me you're jealous of the kid?" Amber answered, feigning surprise and pleased to know he was.

Joe laughed at Amber's obvious lie. At least so far, he was safe from the rapidly developing competition of his young nephew.

"Jealous o' anybody wants to git' next to ma' gal," he answered, wrapping an arm around the young woman and pulling her towards him, "an' 'ats a fak'!"

Joe kissed Amber hard on the lips, lust for her always at the ready.

"C'mon, let's get outa here so's you can stretch 'fore I gas 'is car up," he said, releasing her and reaching for the door handle at his side.

"Awww!" she pouted her reply, "guess if I have to leave you I will cowboy."

Joe laughed and turned to look hungrily at the young woman, ready to take her despite the people surrounding them.

"Don't you temp' me," he said, "an' don' ferget' yer meetin' me Sunday."

"I won't forget," Amber answered him cheekily, "but it's gonna be a long wait for my cowboy."

Joe laughed again as he turned to open the heavy car door.

"Damn right," he murmured under his breath, "but worth it!"

Amber laughed and scooted across the seat to climb out of the car behind him. She was satisfied enough by his answer that he would be thinking of her. No matter who might take her place before they were together again.

Joe felt the whisky hit him as he got out of the car. Between the heat of the sun and the shock of the humidity he was suddenly drunk. He placed his hat on his head and steadied himself as the dogs crowded around him. Reaching down carefully he rubbed the ears of his nephews' enormous black lab that butted his legs and demanded his attention. Audrey and Will were chatting a few feet away. Between the dog butting him and the effects of the whisky their conversation was an indistinct buzz in his head.

He turned to see Amber standing beside him stretching lazily in the blazing afternoon sun, and for a moment thought he might collapse. He shook his head and his equilibrium returned, and he breathed deeply as relief from the short spell moved through him.

"Almos' fell on my ass there!" he said to Amber, grinning as the effect of the whisky eased.

"Too long sittin' in the car," she replied, looking at him critically to confirm his recovery, "and then this crazy heat hitting you."

"Yup," he said, smiling to let her know he was fine, "too much whiskey too fas' s'all, but I'se fan' now honey."

Amber laughed, seeing he was ok.

"It's too damn hot all the same," she said.

"Won't be sayin' 'at come Feb'ary," Joe replied, still smiling at her and feeling good now, "be bitchin' 'bout cold an' wishin' fer 'is heat."

"Now that's true," Amber said.

She grinned at him, enjoying his company and hating that she had to leave.

"This heat sure makes a girl wish for a swimming pool."

Joe laughed and thought of the last swimming pool he had seen years before in the hotel at the small city of Prince George, British Columbia. He was on his way to the town of Smithers and had taken a job working for his brother-in-law at his successful sawmill and logging concern. It was the first indoor pool he had seen. Young and adventurous he had tried a swim in the thing, though he was forced to buy a bathing suit. He could still recall the sting of the chlorinated water in his eyes and the stink of it in his nostrils despite the years that had since passed.

"No use fer a swimmin' pool meself," he said.

Joe smiled at the young woman, sad that she would soon leave.

"But could go fer' a dip in a lake," he said, "an 'ats fer' sure!"

Joe was determined to escape the too tight constraints of his family's home that long ago fall and convinced he would not return. He was stunned to find himself miserable after a few weeks away. When the heavy snow melted from the valleys of the mountains surrounding him, he had quit the job and returned to the low hills of his home.

He would sometimes think back to the sawmill job in the mountains and wonder why he left as they struggled to build the ranch. In the years that followed he was unable to come up with an answer that satisfied both his vanity and his intelligence. He was confounded by a desire to leave for the mountains when the leaves fell from the trees. It seemed his life's biggest regret despite the relief he felt at returning to the flatlands of his birth. Joe had been delighted to no longer have the brooding mountains looming ominously over his every thought.

"I'd be happy to join you cowboy," Amber's sweet voice broke his short reverie, "anytime you want to, let me know and we'll head for the beach."

"Mebbe take 'ese boys with us?" he asked, surprising himself with the notion, "be good fer 'em to see a beach an' get away from 'ere."

"I think we could manage that," Amber said, smiling at his paternal instinct, "might do us all some good to get away together."

"Yer probly right," Joe's answer was noncommittal.

He was oblivious to her familial instinct and distracted by thoughts of the long ago attempt to escape the wilderness of his home.

"Boys'd love it fer sure," he said, forcing the memories from his mind, "an' Will ain't seen a beach since 'fore 'em boys was born."

"We'll have to plan a weekend in that case," Amber said.

She smiled at the first sign of hope from the cowboy and proceeded carefully, not wanting to frighten him.

"Audrey has a tent trailer that sleeps six."

"Car pulls 'at?" Joe asked, still brooding over the mountains.

"Easily," Amber replied, sensing he was slipping away, "and you men don't have to work every waking minute of your summer away."

"True 'nuff," Joe said.

He fixed her with a grin as he paused, apparently considering what she had said.

"Do 'em boys good to see how 'at other half lives I guess," he said.

Amber laughed as she saw he was serious. Hope rose inside of her despite what she knew about the well-earned reputation of the bachelor cowboy standing in front of her.

"Let's make it a date then," her voice was urgent, "you talk to Will and I'll talk to Audrey."

"You jus' made a date girl," Joe answered, smiling at her.

He was puzzled to find himself looking forward to a day at the beach with the boys.

"Gonna talk to Will this week," he said, "letya' know on Sunday sound good?"

"That sounds perfect," Amber replied, meaning it and excited.

Though she would have to take a Saturday off she knew Audrey would be thrilled.

"I'll work on a schedule with big sister and we'll do it."

Joe smiled and nodded at the young woman, charmed by her beauty and looking forward to seeing a lake for the first time in years. The whisky had rendered him compliant, and he was surprised to find himself so agreeable. He was relieved Amber didn't ask him to run off to Las Vegas and get married just then as he might have gone right ahead and done it. A weekend at the lake with the boys was a small risk compared to that he thought with a grin. He could easily talk Will into going on the trip if the damned baler didn't give them any more trouble.

"Done!" he said, smiling at her and liking her more than he wanted.

Joe heard his younger nephew tearing out of the shack to greet them. He winked at Amber quickly and prepared to be hugged by the boy, forgetting for a moment the ominous mountains living in his mind. The girls would go after he filled the car with purple farm gas, leaving the men and boys to life in the wilderness. He could then return to the security of the unyielding solitude. Where a man's dreams lived in silence and he was free to consider the choices he had made, for better or worse, alone and in peace.

Chapter Eighteen

Will Parker crumpled two sheets of old newspaper taken from the cardboard box behind the slop pail into loose balls. He placed them into the firebox of the cast iron cook stove. Picking a few pieces of the finely chopped kindling waiting in a neat pile at the end of the wood box he nestled them into the paper. He took a couple of larger pieces of dry split poplar from the pile in the box and rested them on top of the kindling. Will grabbed the one-gallon container of diesel from beside the slop pail and splashed the remaining fuel onto the wood and paper in the stove. He retrieved a wooden match from the package sitting on the shelf at the back of the enameled white stove. Will scratched it to life on the seat of his pants and threw it into the firebox. When the diesel caught, he replaced the cover on the stovetop.

Will placed the soot blackened iron kettle he had filled from the pail on the washstand at the back of the stove to boil. He grabbed the tea pot from the stove's shelf and emptied the remains of the last batch into the slop pail. It was likely made when they left five days ago. He replaced the pot to await the addition of fresh leaves and the boiling of the kettle. Will shook his head and blinked, fighting the drowsiness caused by the whisky.

His brother was outside gassing up the car for the Hardy girl's trip home, and Tommy was almost through putting away the grub. In a moment he'd sit at the table with Davey to look over his latest drawings. After that he could have a sandwich with the boys before turning in for a nap that would end when he got up to cook supper. While it was too hot to be making a fire in the shack, he wanted a cup of tea to go with the sandwich.

They were out of whisky and he could use another drink.

"Refill 'is diesel can 'fore I get up fer supper Tom," he said, his voice gruffer than he meant it to be, "gonna needa be makin' a fire 'fore I get cookin' 'at roast later."

"Yessir Pa," the boy replied.

"Ya almos' done with 'em supplies an' 'at list?" he asked the boy.

"Onna las' bag now," his son replied, "looks like itsol here."

"Best check it agin' 'at bill," Will grunted.

He reached into his chest pocket for the receipt, waving it at his son who was loading groceries into the cupboard at the back of the room.

"Here 'tis."

The boy crossed the room to retrieve it, placing the wrinkled paper on the countertop as he removed the last of the canned goods. He placed them inside the cupboard.

"Make damn sure we ain't payin' fer more 'n we got," Will said, "an' don't make me havta check it agin."

"Yessir Pa," the boy replied.

"Soons yer done you grab 'at baloney an' 'at white bread an' le's hava bite," Will said, doing his best to soften his tone.

"Ahm hungry an' you boys mus' be too seein' how you ain't eatin' 'em cookies."

Will yawned and looked forward to his nap. He recalled the roast of beef that was probably thawed after the trip home in the trunk of the car.

"Take 'at roast an' hang 'er in 'at well 'til I get up Tom," he said, "too hot fer it ta' sit out all afternoon."

"Yessir Pa," the boy answered, "gonna maka' roast o' beef fer supper tonight?"

"Damn right," Will said with a grin, "figured you men'd be 'bout ready to tie into a few pouns' o' beef after eatin' nuttin' but fresh killed paskies all weekend."

"We sure is Pa, an' you want some onion wit' yer sammich?" his son asked, smiling as he looked up from the list, he was checking against the store receipt.

"An' whatabout some Cheez Whiz?" Tommy's voice was hopeful.

Will smiled at the boy, loving him and wondering why he couldn't tell him he did. He remembered the times he'd ached to hear a word of praise from his father when he was Tommy's age.

"Souns' like a plan," he said, "Tommy-boy."

The boy beamed at the remark and the happiness registered on his young face nearly made Will wince when he saw the reaction. Clearly, he had to find a way to talk with the boy or the kid was going to break. He looked away before the guilt registered on his face.

Davey walked out of the bedroom and placed some papers on the north end of the big table in front of the chair where Will usually sat. He looked to his father, waiting for him to join him at the table.

"Zat yer latest drawings Davey?" he asked.

"Yup," Davey replied proudly, "got some good 'uns I think Pa."

Will smiled at the younger boy, keenly aware he treated his sons' differently from one another and feeling the guilt rise inside him.

"Better hava look at 'em then," he said, knowing there was little he could do to change things today.

"An' then we kin' hava sandwich an' a cuppa tea with yer brother, howzat soun'?"

"Unca Joey-pie too?" Davey asked.

"Sure," Will replied, chuckling as he heard the pet name for his brother, "mebbe we can hava cookie or two after a sandwich, howbout 'at?"

"Dats Poifect Pa!" the boy replied, smiling and clearly thrilled his father was home.

Will stepped across the small room and sat in the metal chair waiting for him at the end of the table. He draped his arm across his youngest sons' shoulders as the boy sat on his lap. He chattered about his drawings, which Will could see featured the perspective lacking in his earlier efforts. There was an obvious grasp of light and shadow in the new drawing. He was again impressed by the surprising talent of the untrained boy. For a moment he forgot his guilt as he inspected the new drawings. While he knew precious little about art Will was about convinced that Davey had been blessed with significant talent. He hoped it might be enough to lead him away from the isolation of the ranch. While he was content with the thought Tommy might follow in his footsteps, he nursed higher goals for Davey. As the younger boys' talent continued to develop, the idea he might someday reach them grew stronger.

The life of a rancher in the wilderness was a hard and lonely one, and Will wanted at least one of the boys to reach for something more. Tommy seemed content working with the livestock and perhaps always would be. A boy with Davey's talent ought to go places. Will hoped to give him the chance and as he looked at the boys' latest drawings, he again considered sending Davey to a school in the city. There he could pursue a bigger dream than what had satisfied his father.

"These are real good Davey," he said to his son, meaning it and believing it was true, "gettin' better every time too!"

"Ya think so Pa?" Davey replied, "really an' fer true?"

"I sure do Davey," Will said, and turned to his older son, "you seen 'is latest Tom?"

"I did Pa," Tommy replied, the pride clear in his quick reply "an' es' gettin' better fast fer sure."

"Looks like we got an artist in the clan," Will said, smiling at the dark-haired boy sitting in his lap.

"Really?" Davey asked, pleased to receive the high praise "Me? An artist?"

"Think so my boy," Will answered, "but you'll havta keep workin' hard if you wanna go anyplace wit' it."

"You think I could Pa?" Davey asked, a note of awe in his voice, "go someplace I mean?"

"Why not Davey?" Will replied, grinning at his son.

"Ain't no place a man can't get to if 'e sets 'is mind to it," he said, startled that he still believed the words, "and works hard."

"In 'at case I better work hard, eh Pa?" Davey asked, looking up into his fathers' smiling face.

"I guess you better Davey," Will's reply was sincere.

He was astonished by his optimism.

"I guess you better Davey," he repeated.

"Better throw some tea in 'at pot Tom," he said to his older son, "an' throw a lil' more wood on 'at fire, kettle oughta be boilin' by now."

"Yessir Pa," Tommy replied, "want I should get the sandwich fixins' ready too?"

"Mites' well," Will answered, "ain't gonna get onna' table by 'emselves an' yer uncle be here inna minute an' hungry fer sure."

He watched as his oldest boy removed the lid to add wood to the fire, working the lifter quickly so the stove didn't lose too much heat into the room. He marveled at the boys' deft movements, the strength and coordination that of a man, years older and confidence plain in every action. While he may not be the happiest kid because of his upbringing Tommy had clearly benefited from it. Will felt his guilt ease. He watched as the boy retrieved the fresh package of tea from the cupboard and dispensed enough leaves for a strong brew. He returned to the stove where he picked up the heavy and now boiling kettle with one hand to fill the tea pot.

"Better move yer pichers Davey," Will said to his younger son, "looks like yer brothers' sayin' it's time fer a bite to eat."

Davey hopped off his lap and collected his drawings. He arranged them in a neat pile and headed off to stash them under his bunk in the bedroom. Tommy went to the east cupboard and retrieved four cups. He placed them on the table before laying the sandwich makings and a sharp knife for cutting the bologna in front of his father.

Will smiled as his boys tended to their separate chores without complaint. It pleased him to be home and he looked forward to enjoying a sandwich. He noticed his brother walking from the fuel pumps to join them. His gratitude for the happiness he had managed to secure from a world so mindlessly cruel almost overtook him. Will swallowed hard and cleared his throat before a tear could betray his emotion.

Chapter Nineteen

Joe Parker withdrew the rotary pump from the forty-five-gallon drum of diesel fuel. He raised it until only the end of its fill shaft remained inside of the barrel. To drain the fuel remaining inside of it he turned the handle a few revolutions in reverse. He silently cursed his brothers' laziness. Will had failed to return the pump dedicated for use in the farms' gas barrels from the wagon box where he left it. Joe decided he was too drunk to walk across the yard to retrieve it. Instead, he withdrew this one; painted red to show it was meant for diesel fuel only, from the barrel at his side to fill Miss Audrey's gas tank. When he rose from the nap, he was badly in need of he could return the pumps to their proper locations. There would be no use for either of them through the rest of the day.

Joe yawned. He waited for the sun to evaporate the remains of the diesel from the shaft of the pump. As it did, he replaced the cap on the fuel barrel and tightened it a single turn. The forty-five-gallon drum of purple farm gas was painted with a green stripe around its middle. It sat next to the barrel of diesel fuel, which had been painted with a similar stripe in red. He grabbed the pliers waiting on the gas barrel and used them to remove its cap. Joe leaned over to sniff quickly from the two-inch opening to confirm it contained gasoline. He picked up the top-heavy pump and slid the shaft into the barrel. As he spun the pumps' adapter lock into place on the barrels' spout, he turned to remove the lid from the gas tank. He was eager to get the car fueled.

Joe recalled that Will had taken a couple of barrels out to the west quarter last week. This was so they could gas up the tractor without returning to the yard while baling. Try as he might, he couldn't remember why he hadn't returned the pump to the proper drum here in the yard. He guessed Will was nervous the boys might choose gas instead of the diesel fuel used for making fires while they were away. Joe scoffed at the notion as both boys had been trained well enough to avoid making such an error. With both the barrels and pumps painted to show their contents there was little chance anyone could make that mistake.

As he pumped the purple farm gas into the tank of the car he thought again of the long-ago winter in the mountains. The unaccountable want to return to the flatlands of his birth continued to perturb him. He enjoyed the work of a lumberjack and had gotten along well with his brother-in-law and his fellow employees. While his memory was hazy due to the whisky, he remembered enjoying the company of his elder sister Frances. Their time together had been limited by the demands of the work. He earned more money that winter than he ever had. While opportunities to enjoy it were few, Smithers was friendly and well stocked with desirable young women.

Yet his wish to return home had been overwhelming by the time the heavy mountain snows melted in the spring. Joe offered no explanation to his brother-in-law. He resigned his position and drove almost nonstop the forty-two hours to his home in the village of Hodgson, Manitoba. His parents were surprised to see him. He said little to anyone about his return other than he was more interested in ranching than he was logging. Within a few years the money saved was used to invest in the ranch he now operated in partnership with his brother.

It was a rare occasion that Joe was asked about it again.

Despite growing happiness with the life he had built since returning from the west he was haunted by thoughts of his time there. He wondered still if perhaps it had been a mistake to leave. Building the ranch was a serious challenge. Many times, he thought he might be better off to leave his brother and pursue a future on his own. The two men regularly butted heads over the business. While he made a habit of deferring to his older brother their feelings had often been bruised as a result. Joe considered asking Will to buy him out of the partnership more than once over the years. The nagging memory of the winter spent in the mountains gnawed at him then.

The boys coming to live with them shelved the thoughts. He was much enamored of them and they had changed the experience of living there in a significant way. No longer were the financial and personal interests of the two men, often competitive, to be served by decisions made about the ranch. The well-being of the boys quickly became the first concern for both. The two men collaborated as never before after the boys arrived. Joe smiled as he thought of the highway and the soon to be secured electricity they had scrimped and saved to afford. If the boys weren't there, they would still be completely isolated from the world outside, of that he was almost certain. Instead, they would soon bring the party line telephone system to the ranch; an unprecedented link to civilization Will would never have agreed to without the boys there. Joe shook his head slowly in genuine surprise. The boys had become the engine of growth for the ranch and the true source of happiness for him and his brother.

He felt a twinge of guilt and real sorrow rise.

It was his brothers' separation from his wife; decried in the family and a disappointment to the community, at the root of their good fortune. That one mans' misery should often be the source of another's happiness could never be denied. Though sad it took his brothers' loss to deliver the surprising gain he was committed to the support and care of his beloved nephews.

The sound of the fuel rising in the spout of the gas tank roused him. Joe slowed his cranking of the pump before it could splash onto the side of the car. He partly withdrew the nozzle from the spout, cranking slowly until the purple gas came into view. Then he pulled it out all the way to hold above his head while turning the rotary handle quickly in reverse. When he was sure the hose was emptied of fuel, he hung the nozzle on the head of the pump. He twisted the cap on the cars' tank until it was tight, and closed the exterior flap covering it.

Joe walked unsteadily around the car. He stopped at the open window of the passenger seat where Amber Hardy waited. Her arms were folded on the sill of the window and her pretty face smiled up at him from behind dark glasses. He bent to kiss her, no longer sad to see her leave and enjoying the taste of her soft lips.

"Yer filled to da brim Miss Audrey," he said.

"Thanks very much Joey," Audrey replied from behind the wheel as she reached to start the engine of the big car.

"Drive safe," he said to her, before taking a step back to address Amber, "Ah'll open 'at gate fer youse an' see you real soon darlin."

"Can't be soon enough for me cowboy," she replied before sitting back into the car to roll up the window.

Joe turned away. He passed the black poplar trees east of the fuel barrels, which provided them no shade from the afternoon sun, and headed for the front gate. As he knew Audrey would speed across the yard the way she did wherever she went in the car he walked quickly. Joe held the gate open and waved to the girls as they departed. The gravel dust rose behind them to blow into the fields surrounding the narrow road. As he locked the gate he smiled as the big car swiftly climbed the low ridge on its way back to civilization.

The men and boys were alone in the sticky heat of the Manitoba wilderness.

Chapter Twenty

Will Parker pushed his chair back from the worn kitchen table and sighed. He wiped the remains of a bologna sandwich from his mouth with the back of his hand. He reached into the chest pocket of his plaid shirt and withdrew a package of cigarettes. Will removed one for himself before extending the package over the table to Joe seated across from him.

"Tailor made?" he asked his brother.

"Don' min' if I do," Joe replied, nodding and taking a cigarette.

Will placed the package on the windows' sill above the table and retrieved a wooden match from the red cardboard box waiting there. He scratched it to life by rubbing it briskly against the leg of his pants. Will extended the burning match and allowed Joe to light the cigarette he held before he lit his own. Inhaling a large drag, he deposited the smoking remains of the tiny matchstick into the ashtray on the table at his side.

"Nuttin' finer," he said, smiling.

"Gol'dern right," Joe replied from across the table.

"Gonna nap me," Will said, and yawned.

"Likewise," Joe answered with a nod, "plum tuckered out."

"Long day tomorra," Will said as a grin spread across his lips, "lotta catchin' up to do."

"Be gettin' 'at baler fixed firs' thing," Joe replied.

Both men sat and smoked in silence. The boys seated side by side at the table between them continued to munch happily on the sandwiches their father made. Wrapped in their own thoughts they were oblivious to the cigarette smoke filling the room. They ravenously consumed the first food they had not prepared for themselves in five days.

"Oughta start thinkin' 'bout gettin' at alfalfa cut 'er lef' 'fer seed," Will said, looking across the table at his brother.

"She's lookin' pert' blue awrite," Joe replied, "price o' seed gettin' up too."

"Ol' man Hersh' said sumpin' 'bout 'at," Will said.

He considering for a moment before continuing.

"Mebbe time to 'range a combine stedda puttin' up more hay," he said.

"Could be we make 'arselfs a few sheckels awrite," Joe answered his brother, "might be worth buyin' a few bales if 'at crops' comin' in."

"S'pose a man could saddle up an' take a look," Will replied before yawning again.

"Aye," Joe said.

Will took a long drag on the rapidly dwindling cigarette,

"Wanna go 'fore 'er after balin' up 'at north quarter?" Joe's question was an invitation.

"You wanna go together?" Will answered, surprised by his brothers' interest.

"Saves arguin' 'bout it later," his brother said.

Will chuckled as he considered the good sense of his younger brothers' suggestion. He grinned across the table at him and wondered why he hadn't been the one to think of the idea.

"Awrite," he said, "les' get out an' hava look 'round tomorra evenin', keep 'em four-legged pets from gettin' too fat if nuttin' else."

Joe smiled back across the table at his older brother.

"Souns' good," he said, "probly be a nice evenin' fer a ride anyhow."

"Yow," Will replied, "an' 'em dang pets 'bin havin' a lazy summer cuzza all 'is haymakin', be good to get 'em saddled up."

Joe nodded in agreement as he ground the remains of the cigarette into the ashtray beside him on the table.

"Hittin' 'at ol' farter fer a whal' me," he said, standing and stretching, "lemme know wenya' getta' start on 'at roast o' beef."

"Ya' gotter pard," Will replied, "gonna snooze some mesef' an' let 'er cool off in 'ere, won' be eatin' 'til after dark I reckon."

Will watched as his brother yawned and nodded to him before striding into the back room out of sight. The sound of his mattress springs shortly followed his exit. He was ready to sleep himself though the effects of the whiskey were easing. A nap would leave him ready for the week to come. The roast of beef he would cook upon rising would make a delicious meal for all of them tonight. The leftovers eaten when work kept them too busy to stop tomorrow afternoon would be appreciated. His sons were finished their sandwiches and ate cookies while seated contentedly at the table with him. They smiled happily and the stress of being alone had now left their faces. He sighed, pleased by their ability to survive on their own yet relieved to be home where he could keep an eye on them.

"Y'ul get 'em saddle hosses into 'at barn while we's nappin' young feller," he said.

He looked at Tommy.

"We'll be saddlin' up tomorra'," he continued, "an' need 'em two geldins' methinks."

"Yessir Pa," the boy replied, "kin' I bring Tuffy in 'fer me an' Swee'pea in 'fer Davey an' put 'em inna barn too?"

Will smiled at his son, knowing how the boy enjoyed riding and how much he liked to be involved in the operation of the ranch.

"Mite's well," he said, "youse boys kin' ride out with us tomorra evenin' to check 'at alfalfa seed if ya' want, get 'em all some exercise."

Davey and Tom looked at each other and grinned, thrilled by the idea.

"Gonna get me rig sharped up tonight Pa," Davey said as he looked at his father, "Swee'pea ain't bin rode in a few weeks an' I don' wan' 'er throwin' me."

"Good thinkin' Davey," Will replied.

He grinned at his younger son, knowing the Welsh pony named Sweet Pea would rather sleep than be forced to wear a saddle. She could sometimes be balky, and Davey was often hard pressed to keep the mare under control.

"Cowboy don' needa be getting himself throwed nohow so's ya' bes' get yersef' ready to ride," he said.

"Don' worry Pa," Davey answered with a grin, "I be reddy fer' ol' Sweeps."

"Bet you will be Davey," he said to the boy, "bet you will be an' ain't got no worries 'bout you neither."

Davey smiled and got up from the table, grabbing the yellow bag of cookies as he did and closing it securely. He took the bag to the cupboard and placed it on a shelf before turning to address his father.

"Gonna go play now Pa," he announced, "be washin' up an' gettin' reddy 'fer supper later, k?"

"Youse a good boy Davey," Will replied, a tender smile creasing his face, "be givin' yer ol' pap a hug 'fore you go an' stay outa trouble whal' yer ol' man has 'is nap, awrite?"

"Yessir Pa," Davey answered.

He returned to the table and hugged his father tightly around the neck before skipping out the front door without a word.

"Don' ferget to water up an' get sumore' wood into 'at box," Will said to his oldest son.

He yawned before continuing.

"Be sure you grab some diesel fuel so's I kin' get statted on 'at roast after me nap, y'hear?"

"Yessir Pa," Tommy replied.

"Get 'at roast outa 'at well soons' you get 'em hawses into the barn," Will said, "they been in 'at pasture a few days now so you best take a pail'a oats with ya' out there."

"Yessir," Tommy said, "you want the grey an' that black fer you an' Uncle Joe?"

"Mite's well," Will answered his son, smiling as he anticipated his wish, "but if 'at miserable grey gives you any trouble the roan mare'll do."

"He won't gimme no trouble Pa," Tommy said, "pail'a oats'll hav' 'em eatin' outa my hans."

Will smiled at his son, knowing he was excited by the invitation to join the men. Tommy would have no difficulty rounding up the saddle horses from the west pasture. Will could see how much it meant to him. He looked forward to the boys coming along and knew Joe would be thrilled.

"You be careful alla same," Will said, his voice soft, "me 'en yer' uncle cain' afford to be losin' ar' top hand 'round here."

"I'll be careful fer sure Pa," Tommy answered him, beaming with pride at the unexpected compliment.

"Attaboy," Will said, "you bes' get after it then, cuz' yer' ol' pap needsa hit 'at fart sack 'fore 'e gets 'at roast cookin' fer supper, y'hear?"

"Kay' Pa," the boy said as he stood up quickly from the table, "I'll get to work now."

"Hold on boy," Will's voice was low, "howbout givin' yer' ol' pap a hug 'fore ya' get yersef' back to work?"

The boy fairly ran into his waiting arms. Will felt a lump press at the back of his throat as obvious relief flooded through his son. He hugged Tommy tight against him. He held the boy close for a long minute, releasing him only when tears threatened to fall from where they hid behind his eyes.

"Yer ol' pap loves you Tommy-boy," he said as he released his son.

His voice was thick, and he turned away so Tommy wouldn't see the tears in his eyes.

"An' yer a damn fine son."

"I love you Pa," the boy said, holding his head down to avoid having his father see his face, "an' yer the bes' dad a guy could have."

Without saying another word, the boy turned and strode for the door. Tommy raised his head and straightened his shoulders, throwing his chest out as his father had taught him. Will watched his son leave to tend to the chores. He wondered again if his pitiful parenting skills would be the eventual ruin of his boys. There was little he could do to improve their lot but continue to do his largely ignorant best. If they were damaged by the effort, he had sworn it wouldn't be due to a lack of effort on his part. He cursed the madness that drove him to leave the boys alone in the wilderness while he relieved his shameful malady.

Will stood and looked through the dirty window. He was relieved to be home and looking forward to getting back to work. The field of blue shimmering in the July heat filled the quarter section east of the yard almost to bursting. His curiosity about the alfalfa crop was genuine. Tomorrow they would check the quantity of seed held by the plants now blooming joyously in their hay fields. He felt the stirring of excitement in his belly at the thought of a windfall. They had planted the crop three years earlier in search of better winter feed for their cattle. An unexpected cash payoff would be more than welcome.

Part Five: All Together

Chapter Twenty-One

Tommy stood on the low wood step in front of the old shack beneath the heat of the mid-afternoon sun. His belly was full and his heart bursting with pride. His father had stunned him with his praise, and he remained mildly shocked to receive the surprising affection. It was rare in his life, and he stood basking in the glow of his full heart, too happy to move. A moment later his dog was beside him nuzzling his hand for attention, and he scratched his floppy ears. He was relieved by the company and would tell Puppits about the surprising events when they were alone.

He looked east to the front quarter and saw the alfalfa plants were surprisingly thick with the blue seed flowers. How he failed to notice before hearing the men talk about it was a mystery. The crop was planted for hay and ahead lay a third summer of handling the heavy green bales. They spit relentlessly from the baler in the heat of the summer afternoons, and he was not looking forward to it. That the alfalfa might be harvested as a cash crop excited him, though his reason differed greatly from his father and uncle. To not have to stand behind the baler and wrestle those green monsters would be a treat. Silently he hoped for the price of the curly seed to rise.

He heard Davey attempting to whistle as he fussed among the assortment of tools and equipment in the tack shed a few yards away. The excitement he felt for the coming ride was plain in the broken persistence of his repeatedly failing attempts. Puppits looked up at him, awaiting instructions and ready to do whatever the boy wanted. The damp heat continued its climb through the July afternoon.

"Ya ready?" he asked the dog quietly.

Puppits wagged his tail hard enough to cause his entire body to sway in reply. He cocked his head to one side and fixed Tommy with an inquisitive stare as though answering him with 'Of course'.

"Let's go get some oats from 'at stable," he said.

With a nod of his head Puppits trotted north, stopping after twenty feet to make sure the boy was following him. After confirming Tommy was coming up the trail behind him, he set off again. He was pleased to leave on a new adventure and thrilled for an opportunity to serve his master. Running ahead of his boy he was soon at the stable. He circled the building and went through the hay yard behind it to check for wildlife waiting to ambush his best friend. After confirming all was well, he stood in front of the stable, on guard, and waited for the boy to arrive.

"All clear up here?" Tommy asked him, smiling as he saw Puppits waiting at full alert in front of the stable.

Puppits wagged his tale in response, cocking his head to the side and awaiting further orders.

"Um gonna grabba pail o' oats," Tommy said to him, "an' we'll go get 'em hosses outa 'at wes' pasture, awrite?"

The dog wagged his tail in reply. He looked to the northwest where ridges covered in thick groves of spruce and poplar trees and dozens of small swamps lay between the stable and the distant pasture. Puppits must stay on guard, as the boy carried no bang stick. He would be watchful for predatory wildlife and prepared to defend him. While neither coyotes nor wolves were likely to appear in the daylight so close to home, he would be alert. The protection of his boy was always his first concern. He sniffed the air for the scent of black bear. One of the short-sighted omnivores might be gorging on berries among the nearby swamps. They searched for any protein they could find as they fattened themselves ahead of the coming winter, and generally presented no danger. His master was small in stature compared to them and without a bang stick. Puppits would be watchful while they were away from the homestead.

"Let's go," Tommy said as he emerged from the stable with the partly filled bucket of oats in his hand.

"An' stay close, I don' wantya chasin' a bear cub out an' gettin' me in trouble with 'is ma."

Puppits wagged his tail in response. He turned and trotted down the cattle trail in front of them. It was worn to hard-packed earth from the countless hooves that created it and as easy to travel as a sidewalk. He stayed within earshot of his master. Puppits was alert and kept an eye on the trail ahead as well as the heavy bush surrounding them. He listened for instructions from his boy and stayed close enough to hear them.

Tommy watched as the dog trotting ahead of him searched for signs of wildlife, smiling as he assumed his guarding posture. Puppits trotted a few paces in front of him before stopping to scout the surrounding bush and the trail ahead. He waited for Tommy to catch up, and then repeated the process. The dog had neither been trained to guard nor to retrieve, and Tommy was thrilled as he watched him handle the seemingly instinctive functions. If predatory wildlife came within smelling distance Puppits would warn him about it. The warning would arrive long before anything was close enough to cause him harm.

"Good dog," he said as he reached the point in the trail where Puppits waited, "you keep an eye out fer bears an' I'll watch fer 'em hosses."

The dog wagged his tail and trotted a few yards further down the trail in front of him. He stopped again, sniffing the air and scanning the trees.

"Goin' ridin' wit' pa and Joe tomorra evenin'," he said to the dog, "guess we ain't gonna havta hunt neither."

The dog looked up wistfully as Tommy arrived at his side, the word 'hunt' acting upon him like magic. He wanted to work for the boy, who would bring down the flying birds or stop those that walked with the bang stick so Puppits could retrieve them. He loved to retrieve the downed birds for his boy, and he loved to eat the warm entrails after he did.

Puppits wished his boy had a bang stick with him now so he could retrieve for him now.

"Don't worry pard," Tommy said to the dog as he noticed the look in his intelligent brown eyes, "we'll get back at it soon enuff, store bought meat won' las' long."

Puppits wagged his tail and again trotted down the trail in front of him. He stopped to scout a few yards later, waiting for his boy to catch up before repeating the practiced activity.

The west pasture where Tommy expected to find the horses lazing through the heat of the afternoon was only a mile distant. Though he knew it was unlikely they might run onto any wildlife along the way he was pleased his dog was there to protect him. In the early spring it was necessary to travel with a rifle. Local predators including bear, coyotes, and the occasional timber wolf populating the home range were hungry after the long winter. The protection and warning provided by his dog then was real. While unnecessary during summer it was good practice for both of them. Tommy continued to pay attention to any signals his friend might relay.

As they emerged from the trees Puppits stopped on the point of a low ridge and waited for him to arrive at his side.

"Pa tol' me I was a good son today," Tommy said to the dog as he walked up to stand beside him, his tone conspiratorial, "said I was top han' 'roun' here too."

The dog looked up and wagged his tail, hearing pride in his boys' voice. He sensed great turmoil mixed with his happiness and was ready to share it with him. Puppits licked his hand to let the boy know he was listening. He nuzzled him so he would know he loved him and would protect him at all costs.

"Said he loved me," Tommy said as he looked at his best friend, his eyes filling with tears and his voice thickening, "tol' 'im I loved 'im too."

Puppits pushed his head against the boys' leg. He emitted a low whine and did his best to comfort his young master as he heard the weight of the feelings coursing through him.

Tommy placed the pail on the ground beside him and knelt suddenly to wrap his arms around the dog's sturdy neck. He sobbed into the thick fur as the weight of the powerful emotions overcame him. His body shuddered and he was wracked by the flood of his tears. The strain of his young life was suddenly too much for him. He held fast to his dog and gasped for the breath that seemed to leave him. Tommy was sure he must be choking as he leaned heavily against Puppits. Tears coursed down his darkly tanned cheeks, soaking the fur of the dogs' neck and dripping onto the dirty t-shirt he wore.

For long minutes he sobbed into his best friends' thick coat. Puppits stood and supported him, not grasping the reason for his boys' sorrow and loving him despite it. As he felt the sobs of the boy begin to slow, he wagged his tail. When he pulled himself away to wipe his eyes and blow his nose Puppits licked the tears from his cheeks. He patiently cleaned the streaks of dirt covering the boys' face and neck where the tears had fallen with his expert tongue. Gently he butted his head into his chest to let the boy know he loved him and that all would be well. They sat together on the low ridge in the stolid wilderness for long minutes, alone and depending on each other.

Slowly control of his emotions returned. Tommy almost laughed as Puppits again began the patient washing of his face and neck with his warm and slobbery wet tongue. The dog comforted him, and he appreciated again that Puppits was the best friend he had and knew he ever would be.

"I love you Puppits," he said, hugging the dogs' thick neck again, "I love you an' I always will, better n' anybody or anything, I swear."

He rose to stand beside his dog.

The south wind was picking up and it plucked at his shirt. The horses should be in the pasture beyond the next ridge a few hundred yards to the north. He grabbed the metal pail and prepared to shake the small amount of oats inside of it. The horses would be drawn by the sound of the familiar treat and follow him to the stable in search of more. No pipers' flute could match the lure of the grain upon them, and Tommy knew his task would shortly be complete.

"Let's go get 'em ponies," he said to his friend, "then we can head home an' grab you a bite to eat an' a drink."

Puppits wagged his tail in response. He trotted down the slope of the open ridge toward the next low rise and the stand of poplar trees covering it. The open pasture that lay beyond was likely filled with horses. His boy had recovered, and all was again well, and he was eager to be of service. He loved his boy and could feel the boys' love for him. Puppits knew that so long as they were together, they would be safe from whatever the world might bring.

Chapter Twenty-Two

Davey lifted the stirrup of the three-quarter sized saddle and hooked it over the horn atop the pommel. He opened the silver buckle of the Blevins strap behind the left fender and adjusted it to hang a notch lower. He had been growing steadily if not fast and was surprised to notice his stirrups were too short the last time, he rode Sweet Pea. Though still the shortest man on the ranch he was starting to catch up and he was pleased.

His saddle was mounted on one of the pair of sawhorses occupying the floor of the tack shed. They were hand built from two by four pine lumber by his father. Davey had adjusted the other side first. After retying the hobble strap, he unhooked the stirrup from the saddle horn and stretched it to the new length. He stepped into the leather wrapped hardwood with his left foot and threw his right leg over the cantle. Settling his weight comfortably into the seat of the saddle he rested one hand on the pommel. He placed the other on the cantle behind him and stood, pushing hard on both stirrups to be sure the buckles were closed, and the leathers lengthened the right amount. He seated himself again; satisfied the stirrups were properly adjusted. His knees kept a slight bend that allowed him to stand in the stirrups with his butt out of the seat. They weren't bent so far they would get sore. He climbed down on the left side as he had been taught. The tanned leather saddle would be ready for a long ride tomorrow evening. Davey was proud he could tend to his own tack.

Davey noticed Tommy and Puppits watching him from the step before leaving to collect the horses. He was glad they departed without stopping to talk. He was considering his own thoughts and wanted no interruption. Davey was trying to figure out what he was feeling now that his father and uncle had returned. The men were snoring in the shack across from the shed. Doggits was sleeping by the door in the shade.

Though he couldn't name exactly what was bothering him, Davey knew it had something to do with the men drinking. His father and uncle seemed to be doing more of it, and he knew he wasn't the only one concerned about it. His brother had been doing his best to hide his own worry. Davey noticed his pained expression when the men arrived, and the stink of whisky was plain. No good came from the drinking and he swore to avoid the evil plague when he was old enough to have the stuff.

It was booze that drove his parents apart. It forced he and his brothers to go on the run after his mother fell under its control. He knew that despite being too young to have a clear memory of it. His brothers often cursed the alcohol that destroyed their family and many times he heard the whispers as teachers discussed 'the Parker kids' at school. Davey couldn't recall the events surrounding the breakup of his family as he had then been a small child. He knew there was a link between drinking and the end of their life together. Now he feared a similar fate might await them here on the ranch.

Davey stepped onto the stump of wood he placed in front of the work bench occupying the west side of the tack shed wall. He reached to unhook a three-quarter sized bridle from the nail where it hung above it. It had been bought specifically for use with the Welsh ponies.

His father first purchased the small horses for the boys to ride. They now bred them on the ranch for sale.

Davey needed the bridle for the ride with Sweet Pea tomorrow and examined the headpiece and throatlatch for wear. He checked the cheek pieces where they connected to the bit and the curb strap for freedom of movement. Then he ran his hands the length of the individual reins. Satisfied all was in good order he hung the bridle on the horn of the little saddle waiting on the sawhorse.

Davey loved his father about as much as he could imagine loving anything, and his uncle Joe almost as much. He was afraid the drinking was getting out of hand. The men had been away this time for longer than ever. Despite it being a Sunday afternoon, they had been drinking before they arrived at the ranch. While he wasn't sure he thought it must be the first time they arrived home drunk in the middle of the day.

At least since the boys came to live with them. Neither of them had shown any concern nor shame after being away for so long.

It had raised an alarm inside of him and Davey was afraid of it.

He turned again to the work bench. He leaned down to the shelf beneath it to search among the heavy saddle blankets for the padded red one he liked to use with Sweet Pea. After finding it under the last pile he removed it carefully. He didn't want to spill the other blankets onto the dirt floor. Davey held a corner with each hand and unfurled it in front of him. He shook it vigorously, turning his face away to avoid inhaling the dust erupting from the dry cloth. Folding the heavy blanket once he placed it across the seat of the little saddle.

His tack was now ready.

Davey again tried his best to whistle, imitating his uncle Joe. He couldn't remember what his uncle told him about placing his tongue against the roof of his mouth or pursing his lips and failed miserably.

With his tack ready Davey looked to the shack where his father and uncle slept. He sighed as there was nothing he could do about either their drinking or his fear of it. That he depended upon the men for his survival had not been a concern before today. Suddenly it seemed important, though he was unsure if he ought to be worried. The fear was real enough, and he again swore to avoid the booze when he was old enough to have it.

His brother and Puppits would be home soon, and he decided to surprise Tommy by feeding the pigs before they got back. It would save him having to and no doubt please him a great deal. His brother had plenty on his mind Davey knew, whether it was girls or chores or looking after the ranch when his father and uncle were away. The idea he might relieve a little of his misery appealed to him. Somebody had to take care of Tom. It seemed obvious to Davey that if he didn't do it nobody else would.

"C'mon Doggits," he said as he stepped out of the tack shed door, "les' go feed 'em pigs fer Tom 'fore him an' Puppits get home."

The black and white dog was awake and, on his feet, almost instantly. His tail wagging an affirmative reply he was ready for whatever his young master should ask of him.

Without a further word they set off for the line of granaries two hundred yards north across the yard. The dog trotted ahead, and the boy walked slowly behind him in the afternoon heat. While the sun was now passed its zenith the heat of the July afternoon had yet to ease. A gentle breeze rising from the south had so far not been strong enough to cool the muggy day.

Chapter Twnety-Three

Will Parker removed the polished leather cowboy boots he wore to town and turned their toes beneath the end of his bed. This would prevent him stepping on them when he rose. He rolled onto the goose down quilt covering the lumpy mattress and sighed. Staring at the rafters above he again promised to sheath and insulate the ceiling this year before the snow flew. The sound of his brothers' snoring rose softly from the bunk at the other end of the room. He silently thanked the god he didn't believe in that Joe had yet to begin grinding his teeth. With any luck he would doze off before the noise of his brothers' sleeping routine began. The screech of teeth being ground to dust in his brothers' head was impossible to ignore and an absolute bar to sleep.

Will turned on his side to face the east wall. He appreciated the familiarity of the old bed and was somehow comforted by the odor of the rarely washed quilt spread upon it. He would nap for a few hours until the heat of the day faded. Then he could cook the roast of beef without turning the shack into a sauna.

Though he had never seen one of the Swedish contraptions he knew they had a reputation for being unbearably hot.

The boys would enjoy a good meal tonight. He and Joe would appreciate the roast beef sandwiches they could take for lunch in the fields tomorrow when they returned to work. It was a large roast, and it would take a few hours to cook. He would stoke the fire and spend the time waiting for it grooming the horses Tommy should soon have in the stable.

Will looked forward to the ride with the boys and his brother tomorrow evening. Joe had been right to suggest it. He was grateful for his help with the decision to make hay or harvest the alfalfa. If the price continued to rise and the seed was of significant quantity, they could easily buy feed if they harvested early enough. To wait until later in the season would risk being caught in the rush for hay sure to take hold if the price of the seed kept rising. Avoiding that was crucial if they were to realize a profit. They were in no danger of running short of feed for the winter. This was due to the wild hay available on their property. The quality of it was significantly lower than that provided by the nutritious alfalfa bales. At the very least if Joe was a partner to whatever decision they should make, there could be no arguing over the results of it.

For that Will knew he would later be grateful no matter how things turned out.

The simple joy of being in the saddle was appealing enough regardless of the purpose of the ride. To be in the company of his boys and his brother only made it better. Joe had been his closest friend since his return from the terrible war that took most of his buddies. They would spend the evening on horseback together. Will loved to ride as much as he loved anything other than his sons and his family.

He did his best to instill a respect for the western traditions in his boys, and the proper care and training of the horses was part of it. The fact they could generate a small amount of revenue by their activities was a secondary consideration at best. Will appreciated the animals were largely pets. The occasional sale of a saddle broke Welsh pony or a team of harness trained heavy horses offset part of the cost of keeping them fed. It was far from a break-even proposition. Fortunately, his brother appreciated the animals as he did himself. They had not been the point of any of their occasional arguments over the course of ranch business.

The men had been schooled in the western tradition by their father and remained committed to it. The horses were an integral part of ranch operations and a significant portion of their image of themselves. Ardent supporters if no longer participants, they regularly traveled long distances throughout the province to watch both professional and amateur rodeo competitions.

They were forced to hire transportation since allowing their driving licenses to run out some years before in a concession to their drinking.

They boys were brought with them on most occasions to further indoctrinate them into the lifestyle. The brothers considered themselves modern day cowboys in the tradition of the old west despite their geographical location in the west central Canadian north.

They conducted themselves that way in spite of increasing encroachment from the outside world.

As the whisky helped him drift into sleep Will's thoughts turned to his father, a veteran of the Great War and easily the hardest man he had ever known. It was his father who brought Will to the isolated country. He and Joe eventually purchased the lands upon which they ranched from him. His father was a man seemingly born angry at the world. Will grew up in constant fear and remembered few times he was given praise or received a kind word. As the first-born son it had been a puzzling and often painful life for him as a child. He was forced to watch as his father lavished his younger siblings in the family of twelve with a comparatively large amount of his admittedly course affections. His mother, who his father loved passionately and was the only person allowed any control over him, did her best to make up for the harsh treatment.

Will loved her dearly.

That he was the focus of her worry and identified as contributing to her early demise was a guilt from which he could not be absolved. The pain of her loss tormented him still. His siblings went to great effort to make him aware they placed no such accountability for their mothers' passing on him. His father made it plain that his oldest sons' many failings, and especially the collapse of his marriage, were significant factors in her loss.

Will and his father rarely spoke since his mothers' funeral, and he was forced to admit, to himself alone, that his life was happier as a result. Will had taken to thanking his mother for relieving him of the obligation to put up with the man's company. While ashamed of it he came to think of the bitter estrangement from his father as her parting gift to him. No matter how he tried he could not deny it. Her death provided him a measure of relief from a misery endured since childhood.

Will yawned and slipped further toward sleep. He relaxed as the joy of being in his own bed, with his boys close at hand and safe, settled into him. The idea his eldest son might struggle with the same troubles he had with his father crossed his mind. He promised himself he would alter the boys' perception of him. If there was anything he didn't want it was to treat his oldest boy the way his father treated him. Will resolved silently to change his ways. No child deserved to be treated that way. Tommy was a good boy, and he would do right by his son. If only to avoid having their relationship turn out like that he suffered through with his father.

He would start again with Tommy when he woke. Tomorrow would be a new day and he would do his best to treat the boys fairly. He loved them equally, and in spite of the differences in their personalities they deserved the same care. So far, he had ignored the possible effects upon the boys that were the likely result of the difference in his treatment of them. Though regrettable and perhaps even irreversible, he would do his best to change the eventual outcome. He would change his approach. As sleep crept near, he resolved to make things better between them.

As he drifted into the sleep, he craved the south wind rustled the leaves of the trees surrounding the little shack. Will knew the evening would be cooled by the gentle breeze. He would spend it grooming his beloved horses and preparing a meal for his boys. Will looked forward to sobering himself completely and returning to work tomorrow, when a new day and a bright future awaited them. All was well. It relieved him to be home on the isolated ranch with the good men he had devoted his life to caring for and raising. He looked forward to better days that were sure to come.

As the first of his snores escaped a dream of horses running free in an open field unfolded in his unconscious mind. The warm south wind shifted toward the east. It cooled the humid afternoon air and eased the temperature in the small shack. The breeze moved through the open windows beside the bed where he slept. In the dream he sat proud in the saddle, riding herd on a remuda of the beautiful horses that had long been his aching hearts' content. The grating screech of his brothers' relentlessly grinding teeth rose from the bed a few feet from where he lay. Will was by now fast asleep and unable to hear it.

Chapter Twenty-Four

Joe Parker hung his black Stetson on the nail protruding from the wall next to the window he had cut into the east wall of the granary. He sat on the end of the bed to remove his polished western boots. These he placed with their toes safely tucked beneath it. He dragged his leather work boots from where they waited and placed them within reach for when he woke. He was tired and his belly full of the thick bologna sandwich he ate in the company of his brother and the two boys. A nap this afternoon would help avoid a hangover tomorrow. He smiled as he thought of the roast his brother would make for their late supper. It felt good to be home. The idea of a nap alone in the old bed comforted him despite his earlier reticence to part from the woman. He sighed and stretched himself out atop the heavy cotton of the goose down quilt.

Joe rolled onto his side to face the east wall. He closed his eyes, seeking shade from the afternoon sun flooding through the uncovered windows of the former granary. The sound of the boys and his brother in the front room was indistinct. Joe relaxed and looked forward to returning to work the following day. They would fix the baler first thing in the morning. Then they could return to the north quarter, which was overgrown with thick wild hay and delivering a surprising volume of heavy bales.

The abundance of wild hay would ease the decision to harvest the alfalfa. Joe was almost convinced more feed would be unnecessary as they had more than enough to see them through the coming winter. There remained a good supply of oats from the winter before while another quarter section of it was yet to be harvested. They might have enough feed for the next two winters if next springs' rains damaged the hay crop.

A cash windfall from the alfalfa this year would be even more valuable as a result. If the crop came in, he might consider recovering his drivers' license and purchasing a new used truck.

It would save money if he could drive them to the rodeo.

The idea was pleasant to consider, and he looked forward to riding with Will and the boys. The bay gelding was likely to be rank after being pastured for a few months. He would enjoy getting the big horse under control. Joe grinned as he thought of the joy his nephews would get seeing him master the horse. The boys were quickly becoming good horsemen themselves and by now had gained an appreciation for the skill required to handle a rank pony.

Joe enjoyed showing off his skills for them in spite of their rapidly advancing years.

The opportunities the four of them had to enjoy a ride together were becoming a rare treat with the boys now in school ten months out of the year. He was embarrassed to admit he had begun to sorely miss spending time with them. The evening ride would bring him a greater joy because of it.

Looking forward to it would help make the heat of the long day baling easier to bear.

As he drifted into sleep, he thought of the strangely repeating pattern in the treatment of the boys unfolding before him. Joe was surprised and a little angry, though unsure what might be done about it. He was unconvinced that what he saw was real and first ignored it as a trick of his imagination. With the passage of time, he became convinced Will was behaving as their father had behaved with his children. The eldest was held to a different standard than the youngest.

The result of the queer parenting strategy was obvious for all to see save their father.

Will had been a difficult youth who had grown into a troubled man. His brother now shared a relationship with their father that was the envy of no one. Many times, Joe wondered why it could be that Will might wish the misery of his own childhood to be visited upon his son.

So far, he had feared mentioning it to his older brother.

While he functioned as a second father to the boys it was clear, though not a word was spoken, that his role was secondary. He had no decision-making authority over the boys about their parenting.

This he was not troubled by as the awesome responsibility of making choices directly impacting the lives of the two boys frightened him.

He pitied Will for the struggles he dealt with trying to accommodate the needs of the boys while managing his responsibilities on the ranch. To be saved those days and nights of internal struggle was a blessing. Joe many times thanked the god his mother taught him to believe in he was saved the responsibility of raising children of his own.

As he dozed, he remembered his childhood days in the company of his many siblings and his kind and loving mother. She seemed a saint when compared to his harsh and demanding father. Yet despite the relative harshness of his fathers' treatment of the children when compared to their mother a special category was reserved for his oldest son Will. Everyone knew it, including his mother. Many times, he heard his mother patiently upbraiding his father in the privacy of their bedroom for his unduly harsh treatment of their eldest son.

Their bedroom was beside his in the big old house where they lived as children.

He remembered his fathers' replies to his mothers' admonishments. They were hard and surprisingly cruel as he swore his eldest son was wild and in need of a heavy hand if he was to amount to anything. Only rarely did Joe remember his parents disagreeing during the years he lived at home with them. The raising of their oldest son was one of few sore points between them he could now recall.

That poor Tommy should suffer a similar misery in his childhood seemed a damned shame to Joe.

Again, he wished there was a way he could get his brother to see what he was doing to the boy. Lately he thought even Davey was aware of the difference in the treatment of himself and his brother. Joe knew it could mean a bad end to the relationship between the brothers if something weren't done to bring things into line. He wondered sleepily what he might do to help, knowing his brother was likely unaware he was in danger of harming the boys.

Soon it would be too late to change the inevitable result.

As sleeps' embrace took him fully into its arms Joe thought no more of his brother and the boys. His mind floated away to dream of the love of his mother and the warmth and safety of her home. Joe was a child among children as he drifted through the rooms of his fathers' house, playing with hand carved toys and enjoying the spoils of his mothers' kitchen. He was free from the concerns of life and its demands. The remembered joy took him quickly past the alcohol induced daze and into the true depths of restful sleep his body had craved.

The rustling of the leaves in the trees outside the two-room shack went unheard. Joe missed the sound of the rising strength of the southern breeze, portend of the wind it would become later in the day. The humidity of the afternoon subsided within an hour of his falling into sleep, though he would be unaware of this. It did little to ease his sweating in the single bed. The heat of the late July sun as it moved through the afternoon slowly became less odious. The tinder-dry wood of the old shack cooled and shrunk around him, though he was unaware of it. His brother's arrival to sleep in the bed only feet away from his own also went unnoticed. The sound of the boys coming and going from the front room did nothing to disturb his rest.

The birds sang in the trees surrounding the shack and the horses ate in the barnyard located only yards west of him. Joe's rest was undisturbed, and he passed the hours peacefully as he recovered from the days of hard drinking. The sleep was a restorative he knew, and when awakened he expected to be fully recuperated. He would be rested and ready to face the myriad responsibilities of life on the isolated ranch. As he slept, he dreamed that his happiness was very nearly complete. With a little more time, he could make sure it was. Then the boys and his difficult brother would be made as whole and well as he believed himself to be. That all their lives should be full and happy was his strongest wish. He snored gently and dreamed true happiness was within their reach. This despite their lives being led in what his brother most often called a god-forsaken wilderness.

Chapter Twenty-Five

Tommy filled the two-gallon pail with oats from the bin his father had built. It sat against the north wall of the stable in the little feed yard. He closed the sloped cover and latching it after placing the bucket on the ground beside him. He picked up the grain and passed quickly through the stable to open the front half door. To prevent the horses following him in he had closed it behind him. As he stepped out of the barn, he was surrounded by the remuda that followed him home in search of the promised treat.

Tommy locked the stable door behind him. He moved through the assortment of mares, colts, and geldings to pour the contents of the bucket into the first of the low wooden feed troughs. It was thirty paces south of the log built stable. Also constructed from roughly split pine logs, the pair of heavy troughs were about twelve feet long. They were mounted on skids to ease their movement. He repeated the task and filled the second of the troughs before squabbling broke out among the horses surrounding them.

Puppits sat contentedly in the grass at the east end of the stable. He watched the proceedings with little interest save to confirm his boy remained safe. The dog was ready to defend the boy even from the horses he knew were his pets. The long walk out and back from the west pasture had been hot. His tongue hung loose from his open mouth and he panted as he sat, cooling himself. When his boy completed the chores, he planned to have a long drink of water before crawling under the work shack. There he would stretch himself out in the cool dirt and be away from the infernal heat. Though it was increasingly difficult to fit under the old shack and even harder to get out it was a worthwhile effort. It was cool and dark beneath the floor. Puppits looked forward to napping there as his heavy coat caused him great suffering in the July humidity.

Tommy walked through the stable into the feed yard, replacing the galvanized tin bucket on the six-inch nail protruding from the wall above the grain bin. He returned to the stable, this time closing the rear half door behind him. He turned into the stall in the northwest corner of the building. He selected a leather halter from among the many items hung on the selection of nails driven into the log wall. There were a dozen halters of different sizes and two sets of harness.

The leather example he selected was for a larger animal and reserved for his fathers' grey gelding.

He opened the half door at the front of the stable and left it open behind him as he walked to the feed troughs. The big grey stood at the first of them eating oats. He slipped the halter shank around his neck and closed the loop around the horses' neck before he lifted his head. He then raised the halter quickly over his nose and behind his ears when he did. The gelding knew he had been caught and enjoying the oats made no attempt to escape. Tommy buckled the halter closed and led the grey horse away from the trough and into the stable.

He tied him in the first stall, where he had earlier filled the feedbox with more of the oats.

He retrieved a second halter, also constructed of leather and of a similar size, for use with the bay gelding his uncle preferred to ride. The gelding stood next to the mare that foaled him four years earlier. He pushed roughly between the feeding animals, doing his best to be neither quiet nor stealthy. He repeated the process of haltering the sometimes-skittish horse before leading the bay gelding to the stable and tying him beside the big grey.

Tommy selected a miniature version of a similar halter, this one constructed of canvas webbing and intended for use with a smaller animal. He returned to the still happily eating horses and snared his brothers' mare Sweet Pea. He tied her in the stall next to the pair of geldings.

The mangers and feedboxes were built lower to the ground than those used by the larger horses.

He repeated the process and retrieved his Welsh stallion Tuffy, who was the lone stud horse allowed to live among the mares. As the short stallion was unable to breed the larger mares without the aid of a special stall and stand combination unplanned foals were rare. The horse was

Tommy's close friend and loved to be ridden by the boy. He made no fuss at being haltered and tied in the stable next to Sweet Pea. He went to work on the oats that filled the feedbox waiting there.

Tommy stood for a moment and scratched his little stallion behind the ears while the horse ate the grain. There were several chores to finish before his father woke and the day was passing rapidly. He resolved to groom the horse after they were done. He walked out of the stable, securing the lower door with its wooden lock as he left.

"Alright Puppits," he said to his waiting friend, "let's get 'em pigs fed an' watered."

With a nod the big dog rose and trotted along the path leading to the northeast. The granaries, the well, and the large corral were a couple of hundred yards north down the worn trail.

Tommy followed him as his mind drifted back to the earlier scene with his father that appeared now to have been something out of a dream.

To say he had been surprised would vastly understate the case, and he was mystified by his fathers' surprising demonstration of affection. He very much appreciated the unnerving display, and now recovered from the emotions that momentarily overcame him found the memory a comfort. It was the first time he could remember his father saying anything complimentary about him in a long time. And almost certainly the first time he had said any such thing directly to him. Compliments were few in his memory. They were directed to people who had very occasionally commented that Tommy seemed a studious or hardworking boy. His father at those times would accept this notice though he did not directly praise him. The direct compliment and the unvarnished affection he received this afternoon were beyond his experience. He remained both surprised and thrilled to have received it.

Tommy was unsure what his fathers' unbidden demonstration of affection might mean for his future. Though he was convinced for the first time his work on the ranch was not going unnoticed. In fact, it seemed his efforts were appreciated, and his contributions valued, and the idea filled him with pride. He would soon be a man. Rather than escape the isolated ranch at the first opportunity; a wish he secretly harbored, he would now have to consider staying. Only hours before he considered himself trapped. The unpredictable current of his young life had again thrown him onto a path over which he had no control. As usual the world was ignorant of his desires and uncaring of his feelings.

Though it seemed this time it might be a path he was willing to consider exploring further.

With a new awareness of his own value, he walked proudly behind his dog and relished the menial chores awaiting his attention. For the first time he saw the value inherent in the reliable completion of the repetitious and often boring tasks. He looked forward to devoting his attentions to them.

No longer were the always hungry pigs a rock hanging from his neck preventing him from reading his precious books. They were now transformed into a valued resource he was charged with caring for and to whom he would devote his best effort. The wood, water, and fuel he had privately cursed at having to relentlessly split, pump, and carry were suddenly invaluable tools of survival. Only he had been given the responsibility of supplying them on their behalf. He was amazed to discover himself the recipient of this trust.

It was placed only in those who could be relied upon to provide them.

The hunting he had always viewed as a joyous escape from the drudgery of the never-ending assortment of dull chores was now shown to be a valuable skill. The meat he provided allowed the men to continue to work when to be forced to secure food from town would mean the interruption of their labors.

This was unacceptable as it might even mean the failure of the ranch.

As he walked behind his dog the new ideas filled his young mind to bursting. He was distracted by the newly found insight into the terms of his life and the isolated world he inhabited. He was scarcely aware of the wind rapidly shifting its direction from south to east and rising in velocity. The sun irresistibly traversed the blue of the summer sky toward the western horizon created by the tall trees behind him. The day was moving toward its end and he had chores to finish.

Tommy resolved to give them the care they deserved, anxious to earn more of his fathers' long withheld praise.

Puppits trotted ahead of him purposefully. He could tell the boy was changed somehow after the moment they shared on the trail earlier. It pleased him to know he had restored him to wellness.

Part Six: Torn Apart

Chapter Twenty-Six

As he emerged from the trees surrounding the stable into the clearing of the farmyard Tommy was surprised to see Davey. His brother walked toward the granary where the crushed grain fed to the pigs was kept. He held an empty five-gallon pail in his hand and could only be returning from feeding the animals. As it was a chore he did his best to avoid Tommy was puzzled to see his brother with the bucket. He placed it inside the old granary before locking it closed as he turned away.

With only a few yards between them and Puppits having trotted up to nuzzle at his hand Davey knew he had been discovered.

"Watcha bin' up to Davey?" Tommy asked his brother, the surprise clear in his voice.

"Figger'd I'd feed 'em pigs fer ya," His brother answered him with a smile, the embarrassment of being caught in the midst of his good deed obvious, "din't 'spect you'd catch me at it."

"You mean ya' fed 'em awreddy?" Tommy asked, plainly impressed.

"Yup," Davey said, "know'd you gotta lot to do, figger'd I'd give ya a han', zat ok?"

"It's more'n ok," he replied with a gratified smile illuminating his face, "it's a big help an' I 'preciate it a bunch!"

"Yer welcome," the younger boy answered with a grin, "an' it's ma' pleasure to help out."

"Wow," Tommy's voice was just above a mumble, "talk about havin' a great day!"

"Wazzat?" his brother asked, his curiosity piqued, "wattup witchoo now?"

"Aw nuttin'," Tommy replied.

He paused before continuing, wondering how much to tell Davey.

"Jus' havin' a good days all," he said.

He paused again, beaming as he considered his day.

"Good hunt 'is mornin', pa an' Uncle Joe home, baloney sammiches 'fer lunch, horses easy ta' catch, an' now you feedin' em pigs 'fer me,' he said, "kinda hard ta' beat, you know?"

"Sure bin' a good one awrite," Davey said, "gonna be a good feed later too."

"Fer' sure," Tommy answered, "an' I'm gonna get wood an' water right now since you got 'em pigs fed fer' me. An' thanks agin' Dave."

"Yer welcome agin' Tom," Davey said, proud to be addressed with the 'adult' version of his name and using the short version of his brothers' in reply.

"Ya min' if I get in some swing time now?" he asked hopefully, "or ya' want me ta' give ya' a han'?"

"You go 'head an' enjoy 'at swing," Tommy replied, "I'll getta rest of 'em chores done quick 'fore I tend to my tack fer tomorra."

"Souns' good," his brother said, "got mine figgered' out while you an' Puppits was gone."

"Good fer' you," Tommy answered.

His brother had impressed him again and he looked at him with new respect.

"A man hasta take care o' 'is tack fer' 'imself don't he?"

"Yup," Davey replied with pride clear in his voice.

His brother had paid him a high compliment and he was pleased to receive it.

"Leas'ways 'ats what pa an' Uncle Joe says."

"They gonna be impressed ya got it straightened away on yer' own Dave," Tommy said, "an' I'm gonna tell 'em you did it yerself too if ya' don' mind."

"Ya' kin' tell 'em if they ask," Davey answered his brother, "ain't no big deal if 'ey don't, jus' wanted to get it done on ma' owns' all."

Tommy was impressed by his younger brother and made no further reply as they walked beside one another toward the shack. When they reached the stand of large black poplar trees next to the fuel drums Davey turned away. A rope swing hung between two trees at the south end of the little grove.

"Be careful 'o that ol' thing," Tommy said.

His brother walked over to unhook the ropes of the swing hanging from a nail driven into one of the trees.

"Will do," Davey replied, "an' you too."

As he walked toward the shack Tommy recalled the nightmare that unfolded with the swing. It happened the first summer they lived on the ranch with their father and uncle. The swing was built by resting a heavy rail on the branches of two large trees and nailing it in place. A length of rope was then attached to form a loop that hung within a foot and a half of the ground. His father had cut a pair of notches into the end of a twelve-inch length of two by eight lumber to serve as a seat. A swing the boys could play on to their hearts' content was made. It was at once a source of great fun, and they spent many an hour competing to see who could swing themselves the highest on it.

Their father had insisted they limit play on the new toy to times when either he or their uncle was present. This was to make sure the boys didn't hurt themselves. When the men planned to be in the fields, they made sure the boys couldn't get at the swing. They did this by hooking the swing's rope behind a rusted iron pulp hook driven into the trunk of the tree serving as one of its poles. The rope was then several feet higher than either of the boys could reach to unhook it.

That they would be prevented from playing on the swing when they were alone quickly became a source of misery for the boys. Only two weeks after it was built the boys had together decided they should be allowed to use it whenever they wanted. They also decided they didn't need any help to keep themselves safe while doing so. A day after making the decision, which was not shared with either their father or Uncle Joe, they set out to free the swings' rope from behind the hook. Within an hour of the men leaving for work they confronted the evil device that held the swing hostage. It taunted them from high above their heads on the trunk of the big tree.

It was a glorious summer morning. Davey retrieved the seat from the foot of the north tree serving as a swing pole. Tommy took hold of the rope hanging from the pulp hook driven into the trunk of the southern tree. Reaching as high as he could above his head, he was just able to grasp the looped end of it. He flipped it vigorously, hoping to dislodge it from behind the hook so they could play on the swing. His attention focused only on his aim; he didn't notice the heavy pulp hook being loosened by his repeated tugging on the rope so far above his head. When he gave a mighty tug, he was sure would free it the hook was instead violently dislodged from the tree trunk above him.

The rusty hook, made of cast iron and heavy, executed a full revolution before the point struck him squarely on the crown of the head.

For an instant both boys stood silent. Davey was stunned by what he had seen. Tommy was shocked by the pain emanating from where the pulp hook had impacted his now fiercely bleeding head. A moment later the heavy iron hook, which for a long second had seemed lodged atop Tommy's skull, fell to the ground. As blood poured from the wound both boys howled, one from pain and the other from fright.

They were saved by a broken Pullman arm. The mower their father had been using was useless without it and he was forced to return to the yard to fix it. Will's shock at being greeted by his sons bawling in stark terror; the elder covered in blood, had nearly caused him a heart attack.

The wound was deep enough to show his sons' skull. After he cleaned it thoroughly with warm water and doused it liberally with iodine it ceased to bleed. Will decided Tommy wasn't injured seriously enough to need hospitalization. Tommy was relieved by the news. The thought of being locked away in hospital was more frightening to him than either the sting of the iodine or the pain of the deep cut itself. He had thanked his father for not making him go. Both boys then informed their father they had been taught an important lesson by what happened. Will didn't return to work that day, instead spending the balance of it keeping an eye on his oldest son. Though he woke Tommy every few hours during the night after the incident no further word was ever spoken about it.

The boys never again attempted to play on the swing without their father or uncle present. They were given permission to do so the next summer. The pulp hook that injured Tommy was replaced by a six-inch nail driven securely into the trunk of the tree.

While his brother still regularly played on the swing, Tommy had lost much of his interest in it after he was injured. Only rarely would he do more than give his brother a push on the thing although he would never admit to being afraid of it.

He walked into the shack and retrieved the fuel pail. It was a half–gallon bucket with spout and handle meant for watering tomato plants and stored behind the slop pail. He noted the slop was almost ready to be emptied and made a mental note to do so when he returned with the diesel fuel. He closed the door behind him and headed for the barrels of fuel standing next to the swing.

Davey was on it now and clearly enjoying himself.

With his boy now busy with chores that would keep them both at home Puppits walked to the water dishes. They waited in the shade on the east side of the tack shed. He noisily lapped a long drink from the near bowl. The remains of the dry food waiting in his dish next to the water and what remained in Doggits dish was soon devoured. He yawned and walked to the open door of the work shack only feet away from the front door of his boys' home.

While the older dog preferred to lie in the tack shed, he liked the cool of the dirt beneath the floor of the work shack.

By lowering his belly as close to the ground as possible he was able, only barely, to squeeze himself beneath the lowest step in front of the shack. He then crawled into the cool of a small pit he had dug in the shade beneath it. This was where he went to escape the heat of the summer. Here he rested himself from the long days and the many chores he and his boy were responsible for completing. It was increasingly difficult to get out of the tiny space as he grew older. He was a stubborn fellow and saw no reason not to rest in his preferred location despite the effort. He sighed as he stretched himself carefully into the dirt. His ribs now almost touched the floorboards above him.

Soon he drifted into a deep sleep.

Tommy unhooked the hose from the red painted diesel pump and held it in the fuel bucket he had placed on top of the forty-five-gallon barrel. He turned the rotating handle rapidly to fill it. He was in a hurry to tend to the remaining chores so he would have them finished before his father woke.

The smell of gasoline rose from the small bucket. The freshening wind, still warm and now coming straight out of the east, blew the scent quickly away from where he stood next to the barrel.

The small bucket was soon filled, and he turned the handle quickly in reverse. He then hooked the spout of the hose into the head of the pump. He would return it to the spot behind the slop pail in the shack. It was a long walk to the well. There he could get a bucket of fresh water and the meat he had placed into a covered pail and hung inside the shaft. He had still to fill the wood box and empty the slop pail before his chores were done. He would have to hurry to finish before his father rose from his nap.

The wind continued to strengthen from the east as he walked to the shack with the bucket of fuel in his hand. Only the rustling of the leaves in the trees and the rhythmic squeak made by the ropes of the old swing disturbed the silence of the implacable wilderness. The wind would cool the evening he knew, and he licked his lips thinking of the delicious roast his father planned to cook for their supper.

It had been a good day so far, and Tommy smiled as he looked ahead to what would surely be an even better evening for all of them.

Chapter Twenty-Seven

Davey leaned back as the swing reached the highest point of its forward travel. He gripped the thick ropes on either side of the wooden seat with all his strength. The weight of his body he used to create more momentum for the return trip. He was crazy about the old swing. While disappointed his brother wouldn't play on it with him save for the odd time and not for long, he continued to enjoy it. He loved the feel of the air passing over him as he cut through it on the end of the rope, and believed it was like flying.

Though he had neither flown nor seen a real airplane he was sure it must be the same.

The memory of his brothers' injury caused by the old pulp hook and their refusal to listen to their father, though faded, remained with him. Despite his joy he was on guard when playing on the swing. It had proven to be a dangerous toy if used without respect. He fell from it several times since his brother had been wounded by the pulp hook. On at least three occasions he suffered injuries of increasing seriousness.

They injuries were the direct result of throwing himself off the swing when it reached the highest point of its travel.

This he did so he might further investigate the theory of flight. As he moved through the air on the swing it fired his imagination. He was convinced there must be a connection between flying and the air passing over and around him. Davey investigated the idea by swinging as high as he could on the squeaky ropes of the old swing.

He had been unable to pull off a moment of actual flight. No matter how high he threw himself nor how fast he traveled when he flung himself free of the seat. The injuries suffered during the failed attempts had yet to dull his fascination with the study. He was just as likely to launch himself out of the seat for the simple joy of feeling the air against his body.

Davey regularly dreamed of flying.

Something about the act of throwing himself into the air, free of constraint and without attachment, soothed an ache he sometimes felt. It was something inside he could neither name nor escape. That he might fly was not his real purpose. To be free for those seconds he was in the air was a balm he had been unable to get from anything else. There were times when he simply craved the relief of it. Today being one of those days surprised him, and as he swung himself higher and faster, he wondered at the possible reasons for it. His last try at achieving flight had left a badly barked left knee that was yet to heal.

Davey didn't want to make it any worse if he could keep from doing so.

The sound of his brother pumping diesel fuel from the fuel drums behind him drifted up as he swung higher and faster. He knew his brother would soon finish his chores and their father shortly awaken from his nap to prepare the evening meal. The idea of eating appealed to him as it always did. He was pleased the men were home and he and Tommy no longer on their own, of that, he was sure. Yet there remained inside of him a nagging sense of unrest. It was as though somewhere there were jobs not finished and actions with unseen consequences taken. The return of the men would normally have removed such feelings. At least it always had. Davey was both puzzled and disturbed that it had not.

He leaned far back in the seat of the swing, holding tight with his hands and pushing violently into the momentum of his travel. The energy built up for the return course would end with a higher point of travel reached on the forward swing. The warm east wind tore at the cuffs of his pants and the sleeves of his shirt. It resisted his speed and limited his travel, and he grinned as the weight of it pressed against him. Like a living thing it opposed him, and he fought to overcome it by using his momentum and all the strength of his body. He was desperate to increase his speed and break free from the weight inside him. Faster and higher he swung. The danger would come and force him to tear his mind away from the stupid feelings and focus on safety.

Davey swung higher and faster, pushing the old swing to free him.

He felt the ropes loosen briefly and then jar as they momentarily unbound from the rail attaching them as he topped the crossbar. The fear arrived then and was an instant relief. He must now slow down or leap off; else the swing might dump him from the wooden seat and onto the beaten earth beneath him. He grinned as he slowed with each pendulum traveled. The force of the wind eased. The rope squeaked again instead of squealing the way it did when pushed almost to its limit. With the weight of his body firmly on the hard seat and the crossbar now above him he breathed deeply. The worn rope had done its job and he was relieved to no longer be filled with the creeping dread.

As the momentum of his swinging slowed further, he noticed for the first time the wind had risen to a stiff breeze. The t-shirt he wore was almost too light now. The sweat he had raised by pushing the swing so hard chilled him. He was surprised as only moments before the late afternoon had been oppressively hot. A cool evening was on the way and it would be a night when sleep came easily. The little shack would be cooled by the wind and his father would cook them a delicious meal. Together they would be safe in their home in spite of the wilderness surrounding them.

As he slowly brought the swing to a stop and dragged his feet lazily beneath the wooden seat he was warmed by the sun on his shoulders. The breeze from the east cooled his still sweating face. Davey grinned as the opposing elements of nature were shown to him as he sat on the old swing. Though enjoying their caress, he was aware he was locked in an endless struggle against them. The dissonant reality of his young life remained beyond the grasp of his intellectual powers. Yet the reality of nature's touch against him was reassurance the mystical forces governing it were genuine.

The east wind blew across the open quarter section before him, and the blue flowers of the alfalfa plants waved a silent dance of response. The falling July sun moved lower in the sky behind him, almost touching the treetops forming the horizon to the west. The domestic animals rested, and the wild birds sang as the heat of the day released them from its relentless grasp. All about him the wilderness awakened to the endless possibilities of the soon approaching night.

Chapter Twenty-Eight

The evening breeze brought Will Parker unwillingly out of the much-needed sleep that claimed his summer afternoon. It blew into the open window at the foot of his bed. While the temperature in the cabin had lowered only slightly the moving wind caught his feet. They were cooled enough to wake him, and he lay for several minutes not willing to accept the nap had ended. Once he rose from the comfort of the bed his life and its responsibilities would quickly reclaim him. He enjoyed the last moments of freedom that sleeping through the middle hours of the day provided.

Will considered the endless list of chores he would need to catch up on after being away from home for the last five days. The length of the list surprised him as he realized being gone so long had caused him to lose ground on the season. He knew well the summer weather, hot and seemingly endless when a man had to work through it, would be gone almost before it arrived. The ranch and those living on it depended on the long days being spent preparing for the bitter cold of the soon returning winter. The days spent away had been a threat to their survival and now all of them would have to work harder to make up the lost time. No cash windfall arriving later in the year would ease their labors. He silently cursed his unfathomable weakness, swearing once more the most recent escapade would be his last.

Will resolved, again, to make good on his promise.

The idea he could make a clean break with his tortured past and a new start raising his sons appealed to him. As he lay facing the uninsulated wall of the old granary, he had converted to a bedroom it seemed an easy enough task.

The essential thing was to have a plan.

He had seen the error of his ways it should be simple enough to change them. He would put right his wrong living and disavow his recalcitrant weakness for the drink. The fractious and divisive relationships he had been developing with his boys could then be repaired. Soon all would be restored to healthy good order. It was plain that discipline was what he needed.

The only thing of value he had learned in the army could finally be put to good use.

Will snorted derisively at the wall in front of him as he recalled the endless bawling of the drill sergeant. The endless drills of basic training were yet to be forgotten.

The comfort of his bed and the nature of his thoughts made him loathe to rise, and he sighed deeply as he again closed his eyes. Work and lots of it awaited him and he was unwilling to face it. The chill of the breeze moving across his sock covered feet was surprisingly uncomfortable, and with a sigh he rolled onto his back. Will stared for a moment at the rafters of the uninsulated roof of the granary above him. With a grunt he turned to raise himself into a seated position on the edge of his mattress.

The lingering effects of five days heavy drinking caused his head to spin when he sat, and he waited for it to stop. He retrieved his leather work boots from beside the bed. Will stood and allowed the nausea rising in his belly to subside before pulling the boots onto his feet. He did it quickly, barely pausing between them and leaving them untied as bending over threatened to make him puke. It was time to make some changes, he thought with a grim smile. A man did himself no good by putting himself into such shape as this. Sooner than he cared to admit he would no longer be a young man.

He stood next to the bed, unwilling to jar his aching head and not wanting to cause the queasiness in his belly to grow any worse. A long minute passed before he attempted any further movement. The thought of cooking and eating held no interest for him, though he knew the boys and his brother would share no such compunctions. With his head spinning only slightly and his belly calming, he turned and headed for the kitchen.

He would make a fire and start on their evening meal as soon as he returned from taking a leak.

Will walked slowly through the front room, noticing Tommy had placed the roast of beef on the table in the topless roasting pan. It was still wrapped in the wax paper it had been packaged in by the butcher at Hershfields' store. He also noted the water buckets were both filled as was the wood box while the slop pail had been emptied. He smiled at the dedicated efficiency of his eldest son. The horses would be fed and waiting in the stable by now. Will was pleased by the discipline the boy had developed from years of living in the wilderness.

Stepping outside the shack he turned to walk unsteadily a few feet to the west. He stopped beside the work shack where he opened his pants and urinated, eyes closed and oblivious to anything save the relief of his overfilled bladder. His head continued to spin as he zipped his fly and turning back to the shack, he crossed the front step and stepped into the noticeably cooler interior. He grabbed the enameled tin dipper from the wall where it hung on a nail beside the water buckets and filled it. Will drained it and one more in a pair of long gulps before sighing with grateful relief.

He took a deep breath, feeling the nagging ache of the hangover threaten him as he crossed the small room to make the fire. Quickly he began the practiced routine, first opening the fire box before retrieving the newspaper from the cardboard box behind it. He crumpled the sheets and placed them into the stove, then grabbed a few sticks of kindling and laid them onto the wrinkled paper. Working by rote now he placed a couple of billets of split poplar atop the kindling. Will took a wooden match from the box on the warming shelf. He held it at the ready before adding a splash of diesel fuel to make sure the fire caught.

His head continued to spin, and he paused before reaching for the can of diesel waiting beyond the fetid odor of the empty slop pail. He closed his eyes and held his breath as he reached for it, hoping to avoid upsetting his still shaky belly. Will poured the fuel into the fire box, silently cursing as he realized he had poured more than he needed. He struck the match to life on the edge of the stove top. Still holding the fuel can in his left hand he tossed the match into the stove.

Will opened his eyes to be sure the paper burned.

What happened next seemed to occur in slow motion and he would be tormented by the memory of it afterwards. While it took less than a second the burst of flame erupting from the stove seemed to crawl up his arm and explode into his face. Shock held him in place as he stood there. It caused him to involuntarily throw the fuel can. The contents covered the wood box and spread the fire with incredible speed. He stumbled away from the stove, wiping reflexively at his singed face. He instinctively grabbed the water bucket and threw its contents onto the blaze covering the wall behind the stove and wood box. Before his stunned eyes the water splashed onto the burgeoning flames and spread them further instead of dousing them. Will realized he would soon be trapped as fire now covered the entire west wall of the little shack. He dove through the light screen door, surrounded by flames. Will rolled across the front steps and onto the hard-packed earth in front of the shack.

The place was doomed, and he was grateful to have gotten out alive.

The terror gripping him was real, and it grew worse as he remembered his brother remained trapped inside the shack. He dragged himself up from the dirt where he lay and rushed as close to the open door as he dared. It now poured smoke and flames were erupting from its roof, to shout to his brother.

"FIRE!" he almost screamed, "FIRE!"

There was no response to his cries from inside the burning cabin.

"WAKE UP JOE!" he yelled at the top of his lungs, desperate to wake his brother before the flames took him, "THE SHACK'S ON FIRE!"

The fire was relentless. Within seconds he was forced to back away from the step as the opened doorway enhanced its ability to breathe. The heat was too great for him to stay.

"FIRE JOE!" he yelled as loud as he could, his voice cracking in terror, "THE SHACKS ON FIRE – GET OUTA THERE!"

Will was forced to back further away due to the intense heat being generated by the rapidly escalating blaze. He heard the unmistakable sound of breaking glass. A pair of boots followed by two Stetsons flew from the east window of the bedroom granary. They brought greater relief to Will Parker than he had ever known. Within seconds another pair of boots followed the hats out the window. A moment later his brother Joe clambered out behind them. His brother was shaken but visibly unhurt and wearing a look of cool derision as he dusted the straw from his shirt. Joe looked back at the flames now consuming their home. The two men nodded to one another silently before turning to gaze at the burning shack. It was being rapidly consumed by the flames, and they were too stunned by the speed of the fire to consider fighting it.

Joe retrieved both pairs of boots and their hats before walking to stand next to his brother to watch the flames growing rapidly in front of them. The blaze had by now spread to the bedroom granary and had broken the windows of both buildings.

"What the fuck happened?" he asked his older brother, who despite having his face and hands singed appeared in good health.

"Fuck if I know," Will replied, noting Joe was unharmed, "went to make a fire an' the sumbitch blew up on me!"

"What?" Joe said, shock plain in his voice, "gas in 'at can 'stedda diesel?"

"Musta bin'," Will said, "howna nama Christ 'at get in there?"

"Be my fault I betcha'," his brother replied, "probly din't change 'at pump after gassin' up 'em girls."

"Ain't 'at a sumbitch?" Will replied sadly, "think 'is fires' gonna spread?"

"Looks like she might," Joe said, "mebbe I cut a hole inna' back wall o' that work shack, get a few tools out jus' in case?"

"Where's 'em boys?" Will asked then, concern plain in his voice.

"DAVEY! TOMMY!" Joe yelled at the top of his lungs as he turned away from his brother, "WHERE ARE YOU?!"

"TOM AND DAVE GET THE FUCK OVER HERE!" Will bawled at the top of his lungs.

The anguish in his voice was obvious and all too real.

"COME ON YOU BOYS!" he yelled again, "ANSWER ME!"

Only a moment passed before the boys appeared. Davey walked from the direction of the swing and Tommy from the tack shed behind the men. Both boys wore looks of fear mixed with relief as they were confronted by the sight of the disheveled men and their burning home. The shack was engulfed in flames that due to the direction of the wind now threatened the work shack only feet away from its front door.

Will was at once relieved to see his sons and again turned his attention to the blaze consuming their home. He was concerned the fire might spread to the trees surrounding the shack and convinced the work shack would be next to go. With no water close at hand there was little to be done. He hoped the fire line created by cutting the trees around the buildings would be enough to keep the forest surrounding the farmyard from catching fire. He noticed only one of the two dogs was in sight, and for a moment wondered where Tommy's dog Puppits was hiding.

The front wall of the original shack suddenly fell away from its roof. It erupted in a shower of flame and sparks to cover the front step of the doomed work shack. Soon the fire was licking up the walls and covering the door of the building.

Will knew they would lose everything inside of it.

The sound of a chain saw erupted from behind the converted granary. Will realized Joe would try cutting his way into the rear of the building to save whatever he could. Almost as quickly he knew that with a strong wind blowing from the east it was the worst possible idea. It would fan the flames now covering the face of the wood building. He backed further away from the heat of the burning shack. He placed his hands on the chest of both of his sons, who stood on either side of him, to take them with him as he did.

"DON'T DO IT JOE!" he yelled vainly, knowing the sound of the saw and the flames would drown out his voice.

"IT'S GONNA MAKE IT WORSE!"

The chain saw roared behind the building. A moment later the sound of the fire gaining strength could be heard following the crash of the wall as it fell. Joe then walked from behind the violently burning work shack, a look of surprise on his soot covered face. He carried the chain saw as he again joined Will and the boys.

Will was glad Joe had given up trying to enter the flame engulfed building. All things would be replaced while his brother could not be, and no matter their differences he loved him deeply. They were safe and that was what mattered. They could certainly build themselves a new and better home than the one burning in front of them. The fire might be a blessing, he thought to himself with a grim smile spreading across his face. A new start might be exactly what they needed.

It was then the howling of the doomed Puppits began.

Will was forced to grab Tommy and restrain him. The boys' beloved dog was trapped beneath the raging flames of the soon to be lost work shack. With hot tears streaming uncontrollably down his stunned cheeks Will knelt to wrap both of his powerful arms around his son. Tommy screamed in unison with his dying best friend. There was nothing they could do to free Puppits. Will knew that keeping his son from being hurt was the only thing to be done. For the boy would have flung himself into the burning building to save his dog. A new bitterness filled Will Parker's heart then, one he could never have imagined. Through tears of rage, he cursed the world and all that was in it. He ached for Tommy as he was forced to suffer the horrifying death of his truest friend.

Chapter Twenty-Nine

Joe Parker dreamed of a life along the cool banks of the Fisher River he had never known as he lay snoring in his bed. His sleep was undisturbed by the east wind blowing into the open window at the foot of his lumpy mattress. In the dream he was building the home his brother Will would give to his wife as a wedding present. He enjoyed the company of his brothers and sisters. All of them basked in the warm and loving company of his father and mother. It was an experience he only hoped to savor in reality. The peaceful happiness he felt in the dream far surpassed anything his actual family life had allowed him.

A lush and green landscape surrounded the four-bedroom house. It sat on a hill overlooking the river above a flood plain. The breeze caressing the working men and women was cool and refreshing. The scent of lilac filled the air, and the sound of his sisters' laughter rode on the wind. The happiness on the faces of his parents filled his heart with light and wonder. He floated above the scene, perched on a rafter of the two-story home with all members of the family within his sight. The river seemed to bend with his view, undulating and receding wherever he should fix his gaze, its waters green and gently flowing. His heart soared as the sound of his parents' laughter filled his ears. The sense things would be this way forever filled his dream.

The joy was palpable and raised a lump in his throat that threatened to cause him real tears.

The sound of his brothers' anguished voice pierced his sleeping reverie with a suddenness causing him to momentarily doubt its reality. In his mind he struggled to return to the rooftop perch, unwilling to accept the dream had not been real. Again, the terrified voice cut through his befogged mind. It forced its way through the dream and rent his newly discovered happiness. Deprived of the joy he had found and angered to be forced from the comfort of sleep he did his best to ignore the repeated calls.

"WAKE UP JOE!" the voice of his brother cut through his drowsy brain like a knife.

His desperation was clear as was the sound of rising panic.

"THE SHACK'S ON FIRE!"

Joe sprang from his bed as the smell of smoke and the sound of flames snapped him fully awake. He ignored the pleas of his brother as he pulled his work boots on with a preternatural calm that surprised him. A glance to the front of the cabin showed his exit blocked by flames. Without hesitating he moved to the end of his bed and slid his hands into his boots waiting there on the floor. Donning them as gloves he smashed the glass and inner support from the east window blocking his escape. He used the soles to clean the remaining shards from the frame. Joe removed the boots from his hands and threw them out the open window. With the surprising calm impressing him further he grabbed his brothers' Stetson and tossed it out of the burning shack. He threw his own hat out behind it. Next, he picked up his brothers shining black cowboy boots and threw them onto the grass beside the hats. Only then did he climb over the old dresser and through the open window. The heat of the rapidly advancing fire licked hotly at his heels. Joe used the straw bales surrounding the shack to cushion his landing as he rolled out of the burning building. A moment later he was free of the rising inferno.

He stood and dusted the straw from his shirt, knowing his brother would be pleased he had saved his boots and hat. As he strolled to retrieve them, he again appreciated his surprisingly calm response to the disaster. Joe was enjoying the moment despite the terrible events unfolding around him.

He grabbed up the two pairs of boots and the hats lying in the grass. He walked toward the tack shed where his brother now stood; nodding at him to reassure him he was unhurt. The shack was burning beyond the point of saving. While his brother wore soot stains and appeared to have been liberally singed, he looked to be unhurt. The fire was devouring their home. Joe placed the hats and the boots a few paces away from where Will was standing and sighed. He thought of everything they were losing in the fire, resigning himself to not buying the truck he craved this year. He watched the blaze greedily consume their worldly possessions. The idea that it might be time for a new wardrobe brought a grim smile to his face. A new home would be a wiser investment than a new truck anyway, he thought ruefully. He hoped again for the price of alfalfa seed to rise.

After chatting a moment with his brother and confirming the boys were both unharmed, he turned away to grab a chain saw from the tack shed. Soon he was cutting an entrance into the back wall of the burning work shack. The section of wall he had cut away fell into the wooden granary. It provided a draft route for the wind and increased the power of the flames engulfing the building. Joe realized it had been in vain and withdrew to avoid being burned. The fire was determined to take everything it could from them. He shook his head and thought of the cost to replace the tools being destroyed in the little shack. A moment later he was standing next to his brother and the boys. Joe watched in stunned disbelief as their world went up in the still rising flames of the relentless fire.

It was the sound of Tommy's dog Puppits howling through the flames that irreparably broke Joe's heart. The screams of the beautiful dog as he died the horrible death beneath the work shack were forever burned into his memory. His eyes had overfilled with tears and he knelt at his nephew Davey's side. He wrapped his arms around him, pulling him close and doing his best to shield him from the sound. Joe looked up to see tears streaming across the cheeks of his brother Will as he cursed aloud and struggled to restrain Tommy. The boy was screaming incoherently in reply to his trapped and dying best friend. He struggled to escape his father, vainly hoping he might save Puppits.

The newly risen east wind excited the flames that rapidly consumed the forlorn wooden buildings. Soon the little structures were burned completely. They left no mark they had once stood save for the black stain of the scorched earth. Where the fire had been lay the twisted remains of the melted tools the buildings had once contained. The sinking sun moved implacably beyond the horizon created by the trees west of them. The cry of the loon and the song of the coyotes were the only sounds to commemorate the passing of the day.

Chapter Thirty

Tommy leaned with his hands beneath his chin atop a post at the barbed wire fence line surrounding the well in the gathering darkness. The full moon rose slowly above the ridge across the alfalfa field from where he stood. His heart ached and his eyes were swollen from tears he had so far been unable to stop. The faint yelp of coyotes and the distant loons call from Poplar Lake broke the endless silence of the vast wilderness around him. He wiped the tears from his scalded cheeks.

How was he ever to survive in the god forsaken place without his beloved Puppits?

The fire that so brutally took his friend had burned out an hour ago. The smoldering ruins were all that remained of the life he knew. He left his uncle Joe and his brother Davey at the tack shed to await the return of his father. Tommy walked to the distant well alone. It was the first walk he had taken on his own in more than three years. It filled him with a rapidly expanding loneliness that seemed to know no bounds. He ached from the loss of his friend. As he grasped for relief, he was confronted by a limitless void within himself. It was somehow amplified by the sweeping emptiness of the falling night.

His father promised they would search the ruins of the work shack for Puppits when the fire cooled enough to allow it. They would give his friend a proper burial, though the idea of burying his beloved dog had so far brought no peace to the boy. His misery was too fresh to accept comfort. The anger filling his secret heart was new. Tommy was inconsolable. He wanted only for his friend to return and could not accept he was never coming back.

His father had departed for the neighbor Huggins ranch with the tractor and the wagon box. He would use the party line telephone and secure emergency supplies. Tommy was relieved to have the time to collect himself and his feelings. Tomorrow they would rebuild. He was shocked by how quickly his father and uncle dismissed the disaster to plan for the future.

Something about that felt wrong.

The anger that grew because of it was a bitter wrath he had never experienced. It was a strangely unsettling exasperation with a rancorous cast far beyond what he had yet known. While his heart ached for relief and his mind for calm, he was confronted only by the growing rage. He struggled with an overwhelming need to strike out and cause harm. Tommy wanted to act without thought or care toward something or someone, anything or anyone, to relieve the acidic fury filling him.

It seemed the only thing he could do was cry. The tears kept coming despite his shame at being unable to stop them. Davey was eventually overwhelmed by the wretched misery. His tears started when Tommy was unable to stop after forty-five minutes. He excused himself to relieve Davey from having to watch him. After assuring his uncle Joe he would go no further than the distant well he left, and there he stopped to stand in the gloaming. Tommy waited for a relief he had already decided was undeserved.

For the cause of the fire that destroyed their home and the awful responsibility for his best friend's death was his alone. This was undeniable as he overheard his father and uncle say gasoline was mistakenly stored in the diesel fuel container. There was no way to change the fact of the matter. He had been irresponsible and careless, and the result was the loss of the best friend he would ever know. It was also a setback from which the ranch and his family could be years overcoming.

How he was to live with that knowledge confronted him as he stood in the dull glow cast by the rising moon. Like a falling star in the evening sky, he realized the rage should rightfully be directed only at the party responsible for the disaster. He was dizzied by the shock of it. The weight of his insight forced him to grip the post he leaned against with both hands to keep himself from falling.

As the knowledge settled onto him the dizziness faded and his tears slowed, and soon he wiped the last of them away. He had been relieved somehow, though he didn't really know why. After a moment he blew his nose. His head ceased the relentless spinning that came with the fire and the horrific passing of his beautiful Puppits. Tommy stepped away from the post and walked to the troughs beside the well.

He splashed his face with the cool water.

It refreshed him and he took a deep breath, relieved to find a target for the still rising anger that didn't magnify his throbbing misery. He was now sure that trying to fix blame for the twin misfortunes at the feet of his father or uncle had caused his misery. That he should so willingly lie to himself only compounded his grief.

Tommy was relieved to grasp his responsibility and see the terrible fault as it truly was.

He felt better in spite of the horrors of the day. Nothing could relieve the pain of losing his beloved Puppits. Accepting the crippling responsibility would allow him to face the men in his family without a greater shame than he deserved.

For that he was grateful.

As the moon rose above him, he thought back to the nights spent feeding the tiny puppy from the glass baby's bottle. He recalled the happiness of sleeping with the small dog in his lonely bunk. Puppits had warmed him and filled Tommy with a peculiar joy.

That he betrayed the friend for whom he was responsible and had cost his life was a crime beyond forgiving. He must be punished for it, this much he knew. As he stood in the sight of the silently rising moon, he swore to himself that he would be. There in the half-light alone with the terrible thoughts Tommy made his decision.

The death of his friend could never be undone. His loss was permanent and so too must be the sentence he should serve as penance. If he were to be redeemed, he must repay the love and grace of his innocent best friend. This he would do by seeking the punishment life reserved for those faithless enough to be careless of their loved ones. There could be no other consolation. For there was no other way to make up for the horrible sin he so thoughtlessly committed.

He must suffer a punishment that would fit such a detestable crime.

The moon rose higher above the ridge. The east wind, now reduced to only a gentle breeze, carried the living sounds of the nocturnal wilderness. The humid warmth of the night reached to embrace him. In the stable on the hill west of where he stood the horses slept standing in their stalls while in the pen beyond the well the pigs lay snoring. Each awaited the coming of the morning light. The boy would arrive to feed them only when the sun rose again in the eastern sky.

The summer night approached in silence, unaware of the misery of the boy and ignorant of his decisions. Implacable and unerring it followed the relentless cycle of life and death upon which the world and all its inhabitants relied. From the still smoldering remains of the buildings that had been his home a grey spire of wistful smoke ascended. Soon it was extinguished by the dewy light of the moonlit sky.

Sadness filled Tommy's newly broken heart. It was as boundless as the slowly unveiling stars into which his broken dreams now rose.

END

About the Author

T.F. Pruden spent a lifetime learning to write fiction while earning a living in a variety of occupations. Widely traveled he is a chronicler of the obscure captivated by the never-ending search for independence. Released in late 2015, 'A Dog and His Boy' was his first novel. Of mixed Aboriginal descent, while writing this novel he lived in small-town Alberta with canine companion Mr. Koko in western Canada.

SOLITARY PRESS 2021

Printed in Great Britain
by Amazon